A DANGEROUS NATIVITY

CAROLINE WARFIELD

ISBN: 978-1976075209

This book is a work of fiction. Names, characters, places, and incidents are either a product of fiction or are used in a fictitious manner, including portrayal of historical figures and situations. Any resemblance to actual persons living or dead is entirely coincidental.

Cover design by Claudia Bost at CWB Designs

DEDICATION

To the Bluestocking Belles—sine qua non.

CONTENTS

1

Pounding hooves and frustration drove the Earl of Chadbourn in a fog of discouragement toward an unfamiliar fence line. He rode head down into the wind until an unexpected sight startled him out of his dismals. He pulled Mercury to a sudden stop. The fence looked to be in good repair. *Thank God*, he thought.

Frustration had driven him from his sister's house, but his neck-or-nothing ride across the fields had done nothing to ease his burdens, raise his spirits, or banish his demons. This did.

Can some part of Emery Wheatly's benighted property actually be in repair?

William Landrum, 10th Earl of Chadbourn badly needed some sign of order. In the two months he had spent struggling with his late unlamented brother-in-law's over-grazed estate, falling fences had been the norm. So had unrepaired tenant cottages, sodden fields, and poorly managed pastures. The only things in good heart he had found so far were those that directly impacted the late Duke of Murnane's personal comfort. If it weren't for Chadbourn's nephew, the duke's son and heir—now his ward—the urge to chuck the whole thing and throw it back on the Crown might be irresistible. He longed to get back to his own land.

Will breathed deeply of the crisp November air, leapt down, and gave his mount a reassuring caress along its neck. He bent to examine the fence, sliding his gloved hand across the top rail. He shook the posts to test their stability. He examined the crossbars. *Perfect.* The earl admired quality workmanship; he rated this work highly indeed.

A short walk took him past a neatly pruned orchard. The cuttings appeared recent, done just after last week's hard frost. The orchard could not be on the Duke of Murnane's land. Eversham Hall boasted no such careful husbandry. He had ridden farther than planned. *What neighbors are these?* he wondered. *Sylvia never mentioned them, but then, my sister doesn't tell me much these days.*

The fence turned at a lane and curved past the orchard. Still leading Mercury, he let his curiosity pull him along until a farmhouse came into view. He stood at the top of a gentle slope looking down at a trim, thatched cottage, solid barn, and garden beds, neat even in late fall, the dried remnants of flowers to the front of the cottage, vegetable patch out behind.

In five years of marching through mud and blood, dreams of just such a scene had been his safe talisman, the peace of rural England keeping the horrors of death and dismemberment at bay. Seeing it in reality, after two months of managing Murnane's damaged legacy, warmed his heart.

He walked down the lane bathed in contentment, drawn by the need to absorb the place's serenity and order until barnyard chaos upended his fanciful notions. He had stumbled onto a domestic crisis. He chuckled as he went.

Piglets ran in several directions, while a goat charged up the hill toward him, eyes wide with panic. Two boys ran in circles trying to catch rioting pigs. The more they ran, the more they sent a flock of geese into a frenzy of honking and feathers. A dog barked frantically on one side, only to run to the other and bark more. In the center of the chaos a woman stood, one hand raised above her head and the other holding her skirts above the confusion.

Will's vision narrowed to the woman. Tall and serene, she put him in mind of Athena, striding above the fray to command calm. Intense longing for her serenity, for her strength, and for order filled him. For a moment, he could think of nothing else.

Frantic bleating brought him back to earth. The goat pelted up the hill toward him. He caught the piece of rope dangling from a loop around the animal's neck before it could charge past him. The panicked beast sent Mercury skittering to the side. A hard yank brought the bleater to an abrupt stop, and a gentle hand and soft voice calmed it. He could see that the rope had been violently torn from a longer piece. *There's a story here*, he thought, a smile twitching his lips. He led the goat down the lane trusting his horse to follow.

"ENOUGH!" Catherine shouted. "Quiet." The dog at least obeyed. Her youngest brother, Randy, skidded to a halt and glanced at her sheepishly while he shouted, "Behind you, Freddy. There's one behind you!"

"Frederick, stop this instant and look at me."

The older of her two siblings stopped his gleeful pursuit reluctantly and turned to look at his sister.

"But the pigs, Cath, I—gore!" Freddy exclaimed. His eyes widened, fixated on a sight past Catherine's shoulder. "That's a fine beast."

Catherine spun on her heels and gasped. A man—and a fine specimen indeed—stood not ten feet away. Tall and broad shouldered, the man exuded the unmistakable confidence of the upper classes. Sunshine did interesting things with the lights in his soft brown hair and his eyes... She found herself momentarily at a loss.

"This animal belongs to you, I presume?" the man asked. His deep rich voice rumbled through Catherine's bemused distraction. She looked up at the huge bay stallion following the man as meekly as a lamb, opened her mouth to deny it, but caught sight of the ragged rope in his hands. He had dragged her irritable goat home.

"Yes. Rosalinda. Thank you." Catherine stumbled over the words.

Randy rushed forward to take the rope.

"Thank you ever so much, sir. So frightened she was, I might have had to chase her clear to the road. If she went onto His Grace's land again, the steward said he'd roast her for dinner." The boy chattered while he tied the animal to the broken gate of the pigsty. "As it is, the mother hog is probably halfway to Wheatton by now."

Warm brown eyes held Catherine's. She found herself unable to speak.

"I say, sir. That horse is a beauty, Mr.—" Freddy began.

"Chadbourn. At your service."

Chadbourn? The earl? Catherine looked in chagrin at her third-best work dress with its patched hem and faded colors. The one time someone from that family appeared on their doorstep, and he found her looking bedraggled.

"Chadbourn?" Freddy echoed. "You can't be. They never come here."

The earl looked confused.

"Frederick!" Catherine snapped, coming sharply to attention. "Mind your manners."

Freddy remained unrepentant as always. "Sorry, Cath, but they don't." He looked at the earl. "May I pet him?" He didn't wait for permission, and the horse seemed willing enough.

"Gently, now," Chadbourn told him.

The sound of the geese faded as the birds ran through the barn. It reminded her that the earl also found Songbird Cottage in confusion. He ought at least to know they possessed manners. She looked to her own manners and began introductions.

"Thank you for your assistance, my lord. I—"

"Your vegetables!" the earl exclaimed.

Vegetables?

He strode past Catherine. She turned around to see that the piglets had settled down to root happily among the last of the unharvested potatoes and turnips, just beyond the kitchen door.

Freddy started to run toward them. The earl put out a hand.

"Steady on. Let them think they've outwitted us, and we'll take them by surprise."

Freddy grinned up at the man and mimicked his stealthy moves until they were almost upon the little beasties. In short order, the boys, the earl, and Catherine held seven piglets by their rear legs and deposited them back in their sty, Randy holding the gate so Freddy could tie it shut.

"Th-thank you for your help, my lord," Catherine stammered, wiping her hands on her skirt and to avoid looking at him. *Must he watch me so intently?* "We would have managed, but thank you, all the same."

"That pen will require mending."

She nodded. "Our man-of-all-work will see to it. Frederick and Randolph, you two may spend the rest of the day restoring the hay to the loft. You've undone two days' work."

"But, Cath! We needed a safe landing place," Freddy insisted.

"Nonsense! Get on with it," she said.

"Safe landing place?" the earl asked.

Randy launched into a breathless description of plans he and Frederick had made for a nativity reenactment involving only animals. Rosalinda, it seems, was intended for the part of archangel.

"She's all white, you see. But we had to test lowering her from the loft. Christmas is six weeks away, and we can't leave it all for the end."

"That explains the broken rope," the earl said in a queer voice. "What happened to the gate of the pen?"

"Kicked on the way down. Swung the wrong way," Freddy answered. "Flew out and landed in the pen. Mother sow took offense and whacked right through the gate on a run. Maybe I should fetch her?" He looked around hopefully.

"An all-animal reenactment?" Chadbourn asked in a strangled voice.

"Yes, well, Freddy thought the runt pig would make a good baby, and Bertha," Randy pointed to the dog, "is ever so good a mother, so we thought it might work." He scratched his head. "But we don't have sheep, and I can't see who might be a king."

"Perhaps it wasn't one of our better ideas," Freddy mumbled. "Needs work."

"Apparently it does," the earl said, looking like he was holding his breath.

"Both of you, hayloft now. That sow is too lazy to go far." Catherine cut in. To their credit, they both obeyed.

She stared after them. What on earth could she say to this man after that recital? She looked around to see him biting his lip to keep from laughing. *Amusement or mockery?* She had no way to tell. When he sobered, his question surprised her.

"Did your crew bring in sufficient silage for winter?" he asked, looking at the animals. He sounded genuinely interested.

"Of course. We had a good harvest across the board. Why do you ask?"

"Did most of the county enjoy a good harvest?"

Catherine launched into an overview of yields for the year, crop by crop, compared to the past three harvests for the farms thereabouts. She caught herself in her peculiarly unfeminine enthusiasms and colored. "That's more than you asked," she said. "Do you have an interest in farming?"

He smiled and looked as if he were about to say something, but changed his mind. Silence became uncomfortable.

"Thank you again," she began.

"Tell your husband I admire the condition of your orchard. Your fences are first-rate," he said.

"I-I'm not married," she stammered. "The farm is my father's." Damn the man. At twenty-six, Catherine knew well enough that the age when women married had passed. She also knew that option had never been available to her. She didn't need some prancing nobleman to rub it in.

The earl looked disconcerted. "My apologies, ma'am. To your father, then, Miss—"

"Catherine," she replied, with a belated curtsey to his title.

He waited a moment, but when she didn't add a surname, he mounted and rode off.

2

Will's laughter followed him home. It broke loose as soon as he rode out of earshot and was no longer in danger of offending his charming hosts. *Angelic goat!* He couldn't remember the last time he'd laughed so hard. Mercury trotted toward Eversham Hall while the earl reveled in his encounter with the neighbors.

Even the confirmation that most of the county enjoyed a good harvest buoyed him. He admired the woman's knowledgeable account. It proved he had been right to fire Eversham's land steward. The fool had botched the harvest. He put what little they had harvested in a damaged shed on top of rotting hay. His incompetence forced them to buy feed for the winter. Being right gave Will cold comfort.

His elation dimmed completely when Stowe, Eversham Hall's morose butler, greeted him in the foyer.

"Her Grace wishes to see you, my lord," the old man intoned. "She said to tell you it is most urgent."

"It always is," Will muttered, as he dragged his feet up the stairs toward Sylvia's sitting room. Unrepaired fences paled next to the damage Emery Wheatly had done in private. He had reduced Will's beautiful, vividly alive little sister to a weeping bundle of misery.

If God is just—and I know He is—coals are being heaped on Emery's sinful carcass right now, while I repair the havoc he left behind. That thought sat ill in his belly. He had to pause in front of Sylvia's door to gather his self-control. When he pushed the door open, heavy, uncirculated air and the suffocating smell of lavender and burnt feathers assaulted his nose. Heavy draperies over every window made the room so dim he had to blink to adjust. He longed for the sunny barnyard he had just left.

Sylvia Wheatly, Duchess of Murnane, swathed in black, languished on a chaise lounge, holding a handkerchief to her nose. Thin, pale, and perpetually ailing, she bore no resemblance to the confident young woman who had danced through her first Season just before Will left to join the army in 1803. Upended books and broken porcelain littered the floor.

"Why can't he come when I call him? Doesn't he know I need him?" she complained loudly.

Who, the late duke or me? It didn't matter. Her rant sounded like a tired litany. She craved a man's attention. *Hell, she thinks she needs a man to validate her every thought.*

"Oh, Chadbourn, thank goodness you're here. Fire this woman!" his sister demanded, pointing with an upswept arm toward her lady's maid, cowering in the door to Her Grace's dressing room. The duchess collapsed back against the chaise.

"She is utterly incompetent," Sylvia whispered, her breathing raspy and ragged. "She misplaced my tonic and only found it moments ago. Turn her out without a character." She finished her pronouncement with a dramatic arm across her eyes.

The maid's pleading look tore at Will. He had ordered her to hide the opium-laced tonic. Obviously, she had not been able to withstand the duchess's whining. *How on earth am I going to find a position for a lady's maid?*

Sylvia peeped out. "Is she gone?"

Will sighed. He gestured toward the hall and followed the maid to the door. His whispered reassurance and request to meet him in the butler's pantry in an hour did little to wipe the fear from her face. He would think of something.

"Is she gone?" Sylvia's voice quavered.

"We will reassign her."

"No! I demand she be turned off without a reference!"

One thing he had learned: his sister cowered before the voice of authority. "You will leave that to me," he said as firmly as he could manage.

Sylvia crumpled immediately, and Will's heart sank. "Yes, Chadbourn, of course," she whined. "Do as you see fit." He would rather she showed some spirit and railed at him. Not that he would turn the maid off. He would just have to make sure the poor girl came nowhere near the duchess. That, and find a lady's maid made of sterner stuff.

The duchess lay back with her eyes closed and moaned. "You don't know what I suffer."

Will struggled to formulate a reply. He bit back a harsh rebuke. "Get up, get outside, get fresh air," had not worked in any of the dozen ways he'd worded it so far. Guilt, all too familiar, plagued him. He had failed to protect her during her debutante year. He left her in the care of his naïve parents, who saw only the good in people. If he had stayed, he'd have investigated Emery Wheatly and known him for the selfish rotter he was. He wouldn't fail her again.

A discreet scratch at the door relieved him of the necessity of a reply.

Sylvia ignored the knock.

"Enter," Will said.

The door opened, and a young boy trussed in formal clothing and unsullied linen entered the room, escorted by his tutor. The boy looked ready to choke on his collar. Charles, the new duke, worried him even more than his sister did. The boy acted like an old man—a fearful, perpetually nervous old man—nothing like a child, nothing like the delightful boys who chased pigs and imagined goats as angels. At ten, he had yet to attend school, yet to visit London, yet to ride a horse. The late duke intended him for Eton, but any effort on Will's part to broach the subject with the boy's mother resulted in another outburst of uncontrolled weeping.

"My darling!" Sylvia exclaimed. "Come read to me while my tonic works its magic. You know how your voice soothes me."

"Sorry, Mother. We are in the midst of studies and—"

"Do studies matter more than your mother?" she snapped.

"Of course not," Mr. Franklin, the tutor soothed. "Your Grace's needs always come first." He gave Charles a shove toward his mother.

"Has he finished his Latin?" Will demanded.

Mr. Franklin startled. He had not seen Will, and obviously wasn't happy to see him now. The man had avoided every effort Will made to inspect the boy's studies. *The toady would rather court the duchess's approval than educate my nephew properly.*

"Today's lesson went well," the man replied stiffly, eyes on the duchess.

"Latin!" Sylvia mocked. "Poor boy. Come here, my darling, and comfort your mother." She pulled an obviously reluctant Charles into her arms. When he pulled back, she pushed a book into his hands. "Read to me, my sweet."

Charles looked at it with distaste. Will put an arm around his shoulder. The book contained poetry of the sloppiest, most sentimental kind. "What were you studying?" Will asked the boy.

"We just started the English Civil War, Chadbourn," the boy said sadly, a note of longing clear in his voice.

The earl's lips tipped up. Any red-blooded boy would rather learn about war than read inane poetry. *Perhaps there is hope for him yet.*

"Uncle Will," he corrected, not for the first time. "When your mother sleeps, come and look for me in the estate office."

"Yes, Uncle Will," the boy said meekly.

"What do you want with my son?" Sylvia demanded.

"Did you know there are two boys close to his age living nearby? I thought Charles might—"

"Unthinkable! We do not go there." Sylvia said, chin up. "Emery forbade it. They are not people we wish to know."

'You can't be. They never come here' The one named Freddy said. Will remembered the boy's insistence on it, and the woman—Catherine—reminding him of his manners. *Interesting.*

"Why did Emery object?" he asked.

"He didn't wish us to see his..." Sylvia paused, glancing at Charles. "It is not to be discussed."

She patted a spot next to her on the chaise and pulled Charles forward. The boy threw one last glance at Will and, with the look of a prisoner going to his fate, began to read.

She may not want to tell me why the neighbors are ignored, but I'll find out sooner or later, Will thought. He left quietly.

CHARLES KNOCKED on the estate office door soon after, as requested. "You wanted to see me, sir?" he asked.

Will exchanged a few words with the boy about his studies, encouraging his interest in history. When he ordered Charles to the stables, however, panic filled the boy's eyes.

"I can't!"

"We've discussed this. A young man of your station must ride. We'll take it in stages. I know you can do this." Will had waited two months since the boy's father's funeral. Enough was enough.

Moments later, Reilly, Eversham Hall's head groom, led out the gentle mare Will had chosen for the boy's lesson. Charles backed away sharply, as soon as the horse came near. He knocked a rail off the fence, and caused the horse to rear up.

Terror gripped Will at the sight of pounding hooves. He dove forward and pulled his nephew out of harm's way. "Think before you act, for God's sake!" he shouted. "That horse could have squashed you like a bug."

"I—"the boy choked out.

"What were you thinking?" Will demanded, gripping the boy's arms with two hands.

"Thinking? The beast did not behave as he ought, Chadbourn," the boy said. His voice quivered.

"Don't blame the horse for your careless behavior."

"They are foul beasts, no matter what you say!" The pale face looked ready to crumple.

He's waiting for me to give him a verbal lashing—or worse, Will thought. He dropped his hands. "I'm not angry with you, Charles," he said, when he had control of his voice. "I'm sorry I shouted. Fear made me cry out."

"Horses don't like me," the boy blurted, in a voice that just missed being a whine.

"Nonsense!" Will squeezed his eyes shut. *It isn't his fault.* "You lack experience, that's all." *And this episode will not help.*

"But His Grace, my father, said—"

"He said a great many things that were less than correct, Charles. We've talked about that."

The boy nodded but didn't look convinced. In the end, the lesson was postponed for another day, so horse, rider, and uncle could calm down.

Charles bolted toward the house. The earl ran his hand through his hair and pounded the fence rail in frustration. The sound of a throat being cleared caught his attention.

"Respectfully, my lord, you might be wanting to know about the boy and horses," Reilly said, pulling his forelock.

"Tell me," the earl said curtly. He took a deep breath and tried again. "Tell me, please. I will be grateful for anything that may help."

"Th' boy took a bad spill when he were a wee lad."

"Go on."

"T'ain't my place to say, but the mount His Grace chose may have been a bit too large and spirited for one that small."

"How small was he?"

"It were his third summer, my lord."

"What did His Grace do when he fell?" Will asked, with a sinking heart.

The groom looked uneasy. He rubbed a line in the dirt with his toe.

"Don't hold back now. I need to know. His Grace is gone."

"Shouted at the boy. Told him a duke's son did not fall. Told him—"

"I see," the earl said through clenched teeth. "Did he try again?"

"Once more that summer, but the lad raised a fuss. Terrified, he was. His Grace had him..." The groom looked away.

"Flogged?"

"I heard caned, but I don't know myself."

"Did he try again?"

"Every summer."

"No success?"

"Got him around the stable yard once or twice. Boy's fear made the horses skittish. Horses made the boy worse."

"Let me guess, the horses were not well chosen, and the duke blamed the boy."

The groom looked down. "I'll be getting back to work," he said.

Will felt sick. He had failed Charles, too. It had taken him too long to realize that Emery kept his family isolated, and why. The duke and duchess attended Will and Sylvia's father's funeral, but left quickly afterward. Her responses to Will's letters were stiff and infrequent. Overwhelmed by his new title and responsibilities, Will had bowed to his brother-in-law's wishes.

He should have known better. Abusers cover their crimes in secrecy. Eventually, he suspected Emery censored Sylvia's mail, but the man died before he could investigate. Only then did the full measure of damage become clear.

His mind went to Songbird Cottage and the boys there. Young Freddy approached Mercury, a huge, spirited stallion, with confidence, skill, and no fear. Once again, the idea arose that the boys at Songbird Cottage might be good for Charles.

Still, Sylvia's veiled comments about those who lived there stood in the way. *It would be like Emery to establish a mistress next door. That's what Sylvia hinted. He certainly had more than one in town.* The woman,

Catherine, didn't look the part, however. *Could those boys be hers? She would have been awfully young, but then, Emery always did like them young.*

He walked back to the hall. *Perhaps I should investigate. If the boys are Emery's, the estate bears some responsibility for them.* A thought made his heart stutter. *The boys could be Charles's brothers!* The thought of investigating cheered him. Songbird Cottage would certainly be more entertaining than the rest of the messes he had to clean up.

Besides, I have to find a decent steward, he thought. *Better than decent. My own land is calling me home, and Sylvia can't oversee this mess.* He could ask about local candidates at Songbird Cottage. It was reason enough to visit. That thought was enough to get him up early with a smile on his face the next day. *Perhaps I can see how the animal nativity has progressed*, he thought with a grin.

3

Catherine hummed to herself as she walked around the barn from the chicken coop. She looked over the numbers on her notes as she did. If production continued at this pace, the egg money alone might provide sufficient cash to see them through winter. *If the hens stay healthy. If the foxes stay away. If—*

A big bay hunter trotted down the lane, slowed to a walk, and stopped. *The curious earl is back.*

A flash of vanity made her wonder if she might pop up the rear stairs and change from her work clothes before she was noticed. The earl looked up and nodded in greeting. He glanced at the door and back at Catherine, as if deciding whether to greet her or knock.

Too late. He can take me as I am.

She strode over and curtseyed to their guest. "What may I do for you, my lord?"

"I thought to pay a call on your father, Miss—" he said.

"Welcome, then. Excuse our informality." She opened the door and brought him in. *In a well-run household, a servant would meet him at the door*, she thought. She wouldn't apologize that their one cook/housekeeper had gone into the village this day. *He'll have to take all of us as we are.*

As if in response to her thoughts, footsteps pounded down from the upper story.

"There's a horse out front, Cath. The earl is back!" Freddy shouted, before he noticed their guest and skidded to a stop. The look on Catherine's face was enough to make him recall his manners.

"Oh, sorry, Lord Chadbourn," he said, sketching a tolerably correct bow. Randy, who followed behind him, did the same.

"Welcome, my lord," Randy said, just before his brother burst out with, "May I see to your horse?"

Freddy looked desperately eager. The earl looked disconcerted.

Of course he doesn't want boys handling his cattle. It isn't as if we have stables.

"His Lordship has come to visit Papa. You young men are meant to be at your numbers. Off with you."

Randy smiled at the earl and started up the stairs, watching over his shoulder. Freddy looked as if he meant to argue.

"Perhaps another time," Chadbourn said. "I will be in the neighborhood at least until the New Year."

Freddy looked thoughtful. Before he could wheedle, the earl went on, "Of course, that assumes your studies are as they should be."

"Yes, sir," Freddy said. He plodded after his brother.

"Charming boys."

Catherine tipped her head. *Did he mean that as a compliment?* She couldn't tell. "This way, my lord."

When they turned in the narrow hallway, the earl's arm brushed hers, sending a jolt of electricity through her. She prayed he didn't notice and focused on the door to the sunny room her father had appropriated for his studies.

She knocked softly but didn't wait for an answer. The door opened to the south-facing breakfast room, lined with windows, their drapery pulled back for maximum light. It was, she noticed, as cluttered as ever. She leaned over with a sigh and picked up papers that had fallen off the wide worktable in the center of the room.

"Papa, we have a visitor." "She looked at the papers in her hand and restored them to the correct pile.

Her father sat hunched over the table, pen in hand. He bobbed his head up. "Visitor? It's Thursday, Catherine."

"The Earl of Chadbourn, Papa. Your Lordship, may I make known to you Lord Arthur Wheatly."

~

Wheatly? Good Lord!

The old man rose to his feet, cast a cautious eye at Will, and bowed. "Chadbourn. Of course. You were at the funeral."

Manners failed the earl. *Who is this man? "Lord Arthur" would make him the younger son of a marquess at least—or a duke. Good Lord! Charles's estate might bear some responsibility for this family, but I'm damned if I know what it is.*

"I—" The earl couldn't articulate a single question from the dozen in his head. He turned to Catherine.

"And you are?"

"She's m'daughter," Wheatly snapped. *Of course she is.*

"Miss Wheatly," the earl said, bowing, "We met before, but I missed your surname during our encounter with the pigs."

"Pigs, Catherine?" Wheatly sputtered. "What nonsense is that?"

Catherine colored deeply. Will followed the rosy glow from her cheek down her neck with his eyes, and imagined how far down that blush might go. He forced that unproductive line of thought from his mind. There was a mystery here, and he meant to solve it.

"The funeral, Wheatly? What do you mean?"

"Emery's, o'course. I saw you there with the boy and his mother."

"You went to the duke's funeral, Father?" Catherine looked astonished.

"Slipped in the back when everyone's attention was up front. Hadn't spoken to the bast—uh, the duke, in twenty years, but it seemed right."

Will's head spun. *He called the duke by his given name.* "I can't help but notice the family name. May I ask your relationship to the duke?"

"None I want to claim, and none you need to know," the old man growled. "Is there a purpose to this call?" The set of his jaw made it clear the subject was closed.

"The earl admired our fences, Father. I believe he came to pay his respects." Catherine's voice took on a soothing tone, while Will tried to recall his excuse for calling.

"Fences?" Lord Arthur waved his hand dismissively. "MacLeish takes care of that. Far too busy with my studies to be bothered by such nonsense."

"MacLeish?" Will asked.

"Our man-of-all-work," Catherine explained. She looked jittery. "Why don't you show your work to the earl, Father." She looked desperate to change the subject.

Wheatly launched easily into his obsession.

"Birds, Chadbourn. England is blessed with 'em." He held up a stack of drawings. The subject had been neatly changed, and good manners prevented Will from probing. "I'm finishing the text for my next work. *Birds of the English Farm and Fields* this time."

"This time?"

Catherine smiled and showed him a shelf next to the mantelpiece. Five well-bound volumes in brown leather, a foot high each, had pride of place. Will could see *Birds of English Marsh and Wetlands* and *Birds of English Woods and Brush* neatly lettered on two of them.

"Impressive, sir."

"Mr. Porter will be wanting this one soon enough," Wheatly said.

"You have until after Christmas, Father," Catherine put in. "At least six weeks."

The old man suddenly pulled one sketch from the pile Catherine had laid on his desk. "This one isn't right," he murmured.

Will looked at the watercolor of a black-and-white bird perched on a leafy branch. He didn't know birds, but the painting looked exquisite to his untrained eye. "It's lovely work," he said.

"Wagtail wing bars aren't so wide. And look. Catherine painted his head cocked downward. They don't sit that way. Point their beaks up like some snooty duchess. Has to be right for Porter."

Catherine took the painting with a sigh. "I'll redo it. Mr. Porter wouldn't know the difference or care, but you will. I'll get to it tonight after supper."

Chadbourn frowned. Miss *Wheatley looks weary. Does nothing happen here without her competent touch? She is nervous, too. My presence makes her jumpy. I need to cut this strange visit short.*

"If I may interrupt, Wheatly, the reason I came was to ask for advice."

Two pairs of wide eyes turned to him.

"Eversham Hall is without a steward. I fired the man for incompetence."

"Excellent!" Catherine exclaimed. "Barker about ruined the land."

"Nasty, too," Wheatly scowled. "Th'duke's creature."

Will wondered what dealings Songbird Cottage had with the rotten steward, but didn't voice the question. "However, that leaves my nephew's estate without a steward. I need someone trustworthy and skilled enough to oversee the restoration of the estate, someone whom I can trust. I can't stay here forever. I hoped you might know someone, Wheatly. It would be best if the man knew local conditions."

The old man looked baffled and confused. Will realized his mistake. He had asked the wrong Wheatly. He looked at Catherine, who appeared lost in thought.

"Have you spoken with Squire Archer?" she asked. "He owns a small estate several miles above Wheatton. His nephew, John Archer, manages it. He's young, and Eversham would be a challenge, but he has the skills. He understands the land. You would do well to speak to him. The Squire wouldn't stand in the way of John improving himself."

Her comments confirmed Will's suspicions about the source of Songbird Cottage's order and well-managed operation. His other suspicions about the estate's obligations toward this household would have to wait until he had more information. Clearly, that wouldn't come from Lord Arthur.

"Thank you, Miss Wheatly. I will call on Squire Adams as soon as I am able. Can you see me out?"

He took his leave of Lord Arthur Wheatly, convinced that he looked relieved to have him gone, and followed his hostess to the door.

"Your sketches and watercolors are superb."

His words must have startled her. When she stumbled on the carpet in the hall, Will reached out to steady her, with one hand to her waist and the other to her wrist. He could feel the rapid beat of her pulse under his hand. *Ah, Miss Wheatly. Your heartbeat is as rapid as mine.* He smiled down at her.

A man could get lost in Catherine Wheatly's eyes. Will realized he was grinning like a fool and tried to rein himself in.

"Does your John Archer have a passion for the land?" he asked. It occurred to him belatedly that she might have a sweetheart.

"Johnny? I would say so, yes. He took his uncle's fields in hand when he reached seventeen, and now they are among the most productive in the county. Soon, they may be almost as productive as mine."

Mine. Any doubt Will may have harbored about her farm management disappeared. She had recommended the *second*-best land steward in the county to him. What would she say if he offered her the position?

"What's so funny?" she asked, gesturing him to the open door.

"I was thinking about the boys," he lied. "Your brothers are a delight."

"Do you think so?" She sounded relieved, as if she had feared otherwise.

"High spirited, as boys ought to be, but respectful and disciplined. They are fine youngsters. I am hoping you will allow them to visit Charles."

"The duke? At Eversham Hall?" She said the words as speaking the name of Hell itself.

"Why not?"

"We're not welcome there."

"My dear Miss Wheatly, the old regime is gone. The less said about the former steward the better, and my brother-in-law. . ." He let his words trail off. *Had she been afraid of Emery*? The thought that the late duke may have forced himself on this woman brought bile to his throat.

"Surely you are aware by now that even the servants know to turn us off. Mrs. Cotter, the cook, even refused to buy my eggs when I approached her in the village. Everyone in the county buys my eggs, unless they have sufficient hens of their own."

He had no answer. Several steps later, she spoke again. "Besides, Papa wouldn't allow it. He calls it 'that vile place.'"

"Miss Wheatly, what—"

"I'm sorry, my lord. We don't talk about it." Her words were polite, but her tone squelched his questions.

"Thank you for your hospitality, Miss Wheatly. Perhaps I'll see you again soon," he said, taking her hand and bowing over it. Her blush when she pulled away warmed his heart. With a proper nod of his head, and a less proper grin, he mounted Mercury and left.

Damn and blast the man. She was certain the earl saw them as a ramshackle household.

He catches me looking like a scullery maid, with Mrs. MacLeish gone to town and unable to answer the door. We provide no tea, nor even offer him a chair. Where were your manners, Catherine? Allowing his hands on her person didn't help either.

She knew full well where her manners went. As soon as he pushed her papa about their relationship to the duke, all other thoughts fled. She didn't know him well, but she knew he didn't miss much and didn't let go once an idea took hold.

He's curious, and he's going to stir up a hornet's nest and make Papa miserable. Damn, damn, and damn.

4

Will leapt up the steps to Eversham Hall and walked with purpose to the butler's pantry. Stowe jumped up from the desk, where he had been enjoying a surreptitious nip, probably of His Grace's brandy. He ought to look guilty. Instead, his pursed lips all too eloquently showed his opinion of an earl who stormed into his refuge dirty from road and horse.

The old man quickly shifted his gaze past the earl's left shoulder. "May I assist you, my lord?" he oozed.

"You have been butler at Eversham many years, have you not, Stowe?"

"I had the honor of serving His Grace's grandfather, the seventh duke," Stowe told him.

Will considered Stowe's likely loyalty to Emery, his ingrained belief in Eversham's routines, even the ones Will abhorred, and knew a moment of doubt. Impulse drove him anyway.

"Can you tell me what lies between Eversham and its neighbors at Songbird Cottage?"

"Lies between, my lord?"

"Why, for example, does the kitchen of this house not obtain its eggs from Songbird?" *That should be a safe enough start.*

"His Grace so ordered it, my lord." Stowe clamped his lips closed.

"But why?"

"It isn't my place, my lord, but..." he hesitated.

Will nodded. "Go on, go on."

"The seventh duke knew the vicar's daughter was no better than she ought to be. He went so far as to step aside when he saw her in the village."

"What about his son?"

"The seventh duke forbade his son to see her," the old man said as if it explained everything. "Will that be all?" He looked ready to escape.

"The seventh duke? You mean the current duke's grandfather?"

Stowe found it unnecessary to reply while Will stood looking at an equestrian print on the butler's wall, reasoning it out. Charles's grandfather forbade Emery "the vicar's daughter," and so Songbird Cottage. *Why should that apply to Charles? Is Catherine the vicar's daughter? She can't be.* He tried to remember when the seventh duke died. *After Sylvia's wedding, but when?*

He seized on the one solid piece of information he had. "Who is Lord Arthur Wheatly?"

Stowe looked pained.

"Come, come, man. Speak up."

"Master Arthur didn't know his place," the old man said through tight lips.

"His place?" *He called Wheatly "Master Arthur," as if he knew him as a child.*

"The duke forbade his sons to go near the vicar's daughter, that is what I know." He clamped his jaw shut.

Will no longer doubted that Lord Arthur was Emery's brother. Their father had forbidden *both* his sons to go near the vicar's daughter. One, or both, failed to respect their father's wishes.

I see no sign of vice at Songbird, but what if Emery, for once, had good reason to keep his son away?

More than one aristocrat kept his bastards away from his legitimate family. Will needed more information, and he needed it quickly.

An hour later, he sealed a carefully worded message with the Chadbourn signet ring. Private messenger would get it to London faster than the post, and more securely. If anyone could unravel Wheatly family secrets, it was the Marquess of Glenaire, Will's boyhood friend. Glenaire's discretion could be counted on.

A groom left for London moments later. Will dispatched a footman carrying a request for an interview to Squire Archer soon after that.

Now what? Will had met few men and no women who had as much passion for the land as he. Catherine Wheatly seemed to be the exception. It would be interesting to press her knowledge. It would be interesting to watch her eyes light up when he did. It would be interesting to watch those eyes if he bent to kiss her. He shook his head to clear that thought. *Slow down, Will!*

His impulse was to invite the Wheatlys, father and daughter, to dinner. *Who would object the loudest, Wheatly or Sylvia?*

"You wish to do *what*?" Sylvia exploded when he asked her an hour later.

"They are gentry. They are neighbors. It is merely a thought."

Sylvia sank back on her chaise longue. "I cannot entertain. I am in mourning. I am ill."

Even in mourning, a family dinner is unexceptional. He didn't dare say that out loud.

"Emery would not permit it. He refused even mention of them in this house. They are not received."

"Emery is dead." *God be praised,* he thought without shame. "Who is Lord Arthur Wheatly?"

Sylvia laid an arm dramatically across her eyes. "The old duke forbade that name in this house. We do not receive them."

"Squire Archer receives them," Will said. The squire had responded with an enthusiastic invitation, all admiration for Catherine Wheatly.

"A country squire is not society, William Chadbourn, you know that," Sylvia said wearily. "I can bear no more about Songbird Cottage."

Will sighed to himself. *At least I've planted a seed,* he thought. "You best be prepared to entertain, however. I've invited Richard Hayden for the holidays."

She popped upright. "The Marquess of Glenaire, here? You can't be serious. His mother, the duchess, is the highest of high sticklers. I can't entertain; I can't." The last came out in a long wail.

"I didn't invite the duchess. I invited Richard, my friend." Glenaire might be more than a bit stuffy, but he would not scoff at Sylvia. The more Will thought about it, the more sure he was that the invitation was just the thing to get Sylvia out of this suffocating room. "It will be a small, informal visit, but you will entertain him, Sylvia. I demand it," he said, forcing his voice to sound firm.

"As you wish, Chadbourn," she sniffed. He left her weeping.

It's for your own good. And call me Will, damn it. I'm your brother.

5

Two weeks later, the earl smiled with satisfaction at his likely new steward. Archer, seeing the state of the fields, running soil between his hands and sniffing it carefully, looked thoughtful. He stood with the earl by a rotting fencerow, next to a bedraggled wheat field.

The man rubbed his hands enthusiastically, even as he pronounced Eversham land a "sad muddle."

"It can be fixed," Will said with more hope than conviction. He didn't dare think otherwise.

"Certainly, my lord, but it'll take a few years, four at least, better in eight. In ten to twelve years, there won't be finer fields in England. Four-field rotation, that's the ticket: wheat, barley, turnips, and clover. We can manage a smaller herd of sheep on the clover fields. Songbird, now, they use three-field rotation. Haven't the livestock to take advantage of the clover, but Miss Wheatly believes doing a bean crop in rotation with wheat and barley does the trick, as well."

Will decided to hire him. He had the knowledge, he had the passion, and he was too young for Catherine Wheatly. That last shouldn't matter, but it did.

"Perhaps we can invite Miss Wheatly over for a meeting, seek her advice in planning," he suggested hopefully.

"Brilliant, my lord. She is the best there is." The young man cleared his throat as if uncomfortable with his own outburst. "Some don't see it, but she is," he murmured more quietly. "For all she's a woman."

Interesting, Will thought. *The county doesn't hold Catherine's origins or behavior against her, but they doubt her unfeminine skills. More fools they.*

The two men walked back toward the stables and barns.

"What of the buildings, Archer? Can you take that on?"

"Buildings, fences, tenant roofs. They all want repair. If I can hire the workers, we can fix it. Folks will be glad of the work."

Will thought for a moment. *Yes, I can picture this man, young as he is, overseeing the work. His enthusiasm alone will carry them along.*

"Hire what you need, Archer. You have a position. Can you start a week from Monday?"

"I can start this hour, my lord. The need is great."

"It is that, but we'll expect you to live in. The steward's cottage needs airing, and your uncle will want you to take your leave."

"He will," Archer said, slightly crestfallen. "I'll speak to Miss Wheatly and see if she can join us then."

The two men walked toward the stable yard to find Eversham stables entertaining guests.

"These two came to visit Mercury, my lord," Reilly the head groom said, with a worried look.

The two Wheatly boys looked at him with cautious hope.

"We just wanted to see the horse, my lord," the one called Freddy said. "You said maybe another time, but you haven't been back."

"Hey, John," Randy peered around the earl to beam up at Archer.

"That's Mr. Archer to you, young sir," the earl said. "Mr. Archer is Eversham Hall's new land steward."

"Brilliant!" Randy exclaimed. "He'll be so much better than—" He hung his head. "Sorry, my lord," he whispered.

Archer suppressed a smile. "I'll see you in a week, my lord," he said. He ruffled Randy's hair. "My best to your papa and sister, Randy." He walked away with a long-limbed stride, and a new sense of purpose.

Freddy looked back and forth between the earl and his brother. He sighed deeply and turned his attention to the interior of the stables. "Do you have many horses, my lord?" he asked.

The contrast between Freddy's obsession and Charles's fear cut the earl like a knife to the belly. The boy's words twisted it. A decision firmed and planted itself in his mind.

"Reilly," he said to the groom. "Perhaps His Grace would like to join us in the stable yard."

The man grinned. "He might, my lord, or he might not, but it'll do 'im good."

~

"THERE'S THE NOBLE ONE!" Freddy exclaimed, looking up at Mercury's great height. "He has fire in his eye, too." He raised a tentative hand and let the animal sniff at him.

"He's a great horrid beast," came a voice from the door. Charles stood with his feet planted outside the stable, a footman at his side.

"He's a beauty," Freddy disagreed, spinning on his heels. "How can you say that?"

"He's too much mount for a boy," Will put in before Charles could argue. "Come out to the stable yard, and I will make some introductions." He whispered instructions to Reilly and led the Wheatly boys out to the paddock. Two horses grazed in the grassy enclosure.

Freddy watched them with unfiltered longing. "Bit elderly, those," he murmured.

"Still able to carry a load," the earl told him. At the earl's voice, one of the two ambled over. He fetched out a lump of sugar. "Always know where the sweets are, don't you, now?" He patted the horse's neck and accepted a nuzzle in return.

"Gentlemen, let me introduce you to Lady Guinevere, Eversham's matriarch." Charles looked pained. "But I forgot my manners.

Charles, permit me to make known to you Master Randolph and Master Frank Wheatly. Boys, this is Charles Wheatly, Duke of Murnane. I have the honor of being his uncle."

Both boys made a proper bow, but Randy couldn't contain his interest. "Wheatly! We have the same name," he exclaimed.

Freddy, who had already begun to caress Lady Guinevere's nose, said, "Of course we do, but Papa don't like to talk about it."

Charles did his best to maintain a haughty expression, but curiosity got the better of him. "What do you mean by, 'of course'?"

"I believe you are cousins, Charles. Freddy and Randy's father is your father's brother."

"Brilliant!" Randy exclaimed. "Cousins are almost as good as brothers."

The idea seemed to startle Charles.

"I'm ten just this month," Randy went on without noticing. "Freddy's twelve. How old are you?"

Charles glanced at his uncle. Nothing in his experience prepared him for the Wheatlys. Will could tell he waffled between putting Randy down as impertinent, and responding in kind. He looked at the other boys as though they were some sort of exotics. "Ten," he said at last.

"You're the lucky one, I guess," Freddy sighed, still looking at the horse. He climbed up on a fence rail to get closer. Charles frowned. "You get to have these beauties." *Not the title. Not the house. Not the wardrobe. The horses. Good man, Freddy!*

"Would you like to give the lady a trot around the paddock?" Will asked.

Freddy leapt down. "May I?" he breathed. Reilly came out of the barn carrying saddle and tack.

"Help Mr. Reilly saddle the horse, and you certainly may."

Charles watched Freddy scramble over the fence and take instructions from Reilly with open curiosity, and, Will hoped, some longing.

"Horse mad," Randy said.

"I beg your pardon?" the young duke asked.

"My brother is horse mad. Always was."

"Do you like horses?" Charles asked cautiously.

"I like them well enough, but I don't get much chance to ride. I like all animals. What is your favorite?" Randy asked.

Charles looked perplexed. Will doubted the boy interacted with livestock, much less wild animals. He had obviously had few interactions with boys his own age.

Randy went on talking. "I like the farm animals myself. The pigs smell, but they are smart as can be. The geese are bad tempered, and the chickens aren't too bright. The goat, though, is my favorite. Do you prefer wild ones?" This time he looked directly at his cousin, expecting an answer.

"I like birds," Charles admitted finally. "Especially hawks. I can see them from the nursery window when they hunt in the meadow."

"Brilliant!" Randy said. "I love them. There's a red-tail that hunts in the orchard. We have an owl in the woods, did you know?"

"Truly? I've read about them, but I've never seen one." Will watched his nephew's eyes shine with interest, all thoughts of status and class gone. He bit back his smile.

"I could show you. It isn't far," Randy suggested.

Charles turned to his uncle as if to ask if he might.

"Up you go, Freddy," Will said, putting an arm around Charles. "She's a patient and gentle soul. Walk her easy." Freddy clearly needed little instruction; he was a born rider. With little encouragement from Reilly, he began to circle the paddock.

"I could do that, if I wanted to," Charles said stiffly.

"Of course you could," Randy told him. "It just takes a bit of patience and practice." He leaned in. "Even *I* can do it."

Will thanked the Good Lord who sent these boys into his life. *I might get through to Charles yet.* Before he could consider how best to take advantage, retribution arrived in the form of an irate older sister.

"Randolph and Frederick Wheatly, what on earth are you about?"

"Hello, Cath," Freddy called from horseback. "We're just visiting. His Grace doesn't mind." He put his mount to a trot.

~

His Grace, in Catherine's opinion, looked rather too stunned to mind, if the awkward boy next to Chadbourn was, indeed, the new duke.

"Miss Wheatly, it is my privilege to present His Grace, the Duke of Murnane, Charles Wheatly. Charles, may I present Miss Catherine Wheatly?"

"I'm honored, Your Grace." Catherine curtseyed to the boy properly. Through lowered lashes, she watched his uncle whisper in his ear. The duke looked at Chadbourn in question before he turned back to Catherine. *What on earth?*

The young duke looked uncertain. "Chadbourn suggests you should call me Charles, since we are cousins. Are you really my cousin?" he asked.

Or something very like. "Of course, if your uncle says it. You may call me Catherine, if you like." His returning smile looked more shy than haughty. Catherine warmed to the boy immediately.

"Cath, His Grace likes birds," Randy broke in. "Can I show him the owl in the woods? He don't even know it's there, even though it is practically on his land," Randy enthused.

"That would be 'may I' and 'he doesn't...'" She caught the earl's eye. "I need to discuss it with His Lordship." She couldn't decide if Chadbourn's welcome of her brothers boded good or ill. *The damned man seems amused.*

"Famous," Randy said to Charles, "Cath will talk him round. She likes the owl, too. My father is an *expert* on birds. Would you like to see his books?" The two boys moved toward the rails, talking a mile a minute, but Catherine quit listening. Chadbourn's eyes held hers.

"When would you like him?" Chadbourn asked with a grin.

"Beg pardon?" Catherine shook off the stupor his gaze had engendered.

"My nephew. Nothing for it. He has to visit."

"I'm sorry, my lord. This is all too much. We don't 'visit' with Eversham Hall."

"And that's a damned shame. The boys are good for Charles, and he would be good for them."

Catherine searched her brain for a riposte. Her hard-won contentment lay on the ground. *This interfering earl plans to upset everything.*

"You said yourself, you would only be here until the New Year. You don't—"

"They are only boys, Miss Wheatly. Whatever lies between Songbird Cottage and Eversham Hall need not color their lives."

She frowned but had no reply, because in her heart she agreed with him.

"The horses alone would enrich Freddy's life, and his example might—"

Whatever the earl meant to say was cut short by a screech from farther down the paddock fence. Charles lay half-suspended on a fence rail inside the paddock. Both adults took off at a dead run. Randy had his arms around the young duke supporting his weight. A nasty slice that cut through his trouser leg oozed blood.

"I'm bleeding, Uncle Will," the boy cried.

Chadbourn called out to Freddy, "Help Reilly get the horses out of the paddock!" He lowered his nephew to the ground and tore back the cloth around the duke's thigh. The earl looked frantic. Freddy dropped to the ground and led the horse away, while Reilly ran to help.

"Am I going to die?" the boy asked. His clenched teeth looked like they held back a cry. Catherine guessed he couldn't bear to show weakness in front of other boys.

Before the earl could answer, Randy piped up. "No, but you may get an interesting scar from that one. I sliced my arm on a broken branch last year. Hurt like the Devil, but I got the best scar." He started to roll up his sleeve.

Catherine thought about the days she spent dreading infection, and dropped down beside the earl.

"It doesn't look so bad," she said soothingly, but whether she meant to reassure the boy or his uncle, she couldn't say. "It will need some attention, though. Cleaning and bandaging. An application of honey may be in order."

"Honey?" the earl and the duke asked in unison.

"It aids healing. I don't know why, but it makes infection less likely. Dark is best if you have it. I can send some, if you don't."

"I saw a surgeon use it in the Peninsula once. Does it work?"

She cast him a sardonic eye. *Of course it works, you looby.*

"Ever so well," Randy interrupted. "And Catherine will give you a spoonful when she's finished dressing the cut. That's the best part."

Catherine did not intend to dress it. "Not I, the earl. We're going home. Now."

"You can't. I need your help." Chadbourn lifted his nephew into his arms, and Catherine rose to her feet. "Come along." He started for the Hall, but Catherine stood fast. She stared up at the imposing façade of the old house and felt her stomach clench. The earl turned to see why she didn't follow.

"Miss Wheatly, we need your help. You obviously know more about cuts than I."

Don't these people have servants for that?

"You know more about boys, too, I think," the earl went on.

A boy needs more than servants and bandaging when he's been hurt.

She turned to her brother. "Randy, fetch Freddy, and the two of you go directly home. I expect to find you there shortly, and I'll be wanting an explanation for what happened."

"There's nothing to explain. His Grace climbed the fence after me, and he slipped. It wasn't my fault."

"Home. Now." He left, head hanging.

Catherine took a steadying breath.

"Will you come now, please?" Chadbourn urged. She fell into step beside him, feeling like a cow in the vicar's parlor in her plain dress.

I don't belong here.

THE LINE of a woman's back surpasses the grace of any cathedral, Will believed. *At least this woman's does.* He looked his fill at Catherine bent over his nephew, and smiled to himself. He found her gentle competence oddly compelling, also. They had laid Charles on a sofa in the tradesmen's parlor, while Will had shouted for cloths, hot water, and honey. She had cleaned and bandaged the wound in short order, all the while encouraging the boy and quieting his fears. Her strong hands wrung out the cloths she had used into a basin, before she handed both the basin and rags to a waiting footman and rolled the sleeves of her simple dress back down.

Will watched her smooth back Charles's hair, and longed to feel those strong, gentle fingers in his own. When she kissed the boy's cheek, he felt a wholly inappropriate surge of desire. He ought to be concerned for his nephew, not lusting after his extraordinary neighbor.

"Will I get honey? Randy said you would give me some," Charles reminded her.

"Of course!" Catherine answered with a chuckle. She reached for the honey pot. "You were very brave."

"I was, wasn't I, Uncle Will?"

Will didn't answer, lost in the woman's husky voice. *That voice would reduce a man to begging.*

"Uncle Will?" Charles repeated.

"Yes. You were very brave," the earl murmured.

When Catherine popped a spoon of honey into the boy's mouth, the adoration on Charles's face mirrored his uncle's.

"Chadbourn! Why didn't you come when I sent for you? Franklin told me those horrid boys imposed themselves on Charles. He said you ordered him brought to the stables, but I couldn't believe it."

Will spun around to see Sylvia leaning on the door-frame, breathing rapidly. He saw the moment her eyes found Charles and the white bandage around his right thigh.

"Dear God, what have you done to my son?"

She looked as if she might faint. Will stepped closer, but she proved to be sturdier than he thought. She pushed herself forward and fell to her knees beside her son. Catherine stood and moved away. Will put out a hand to steady Catherine, but she sidestepped him.

"My baby, what did they do to you?" She grabbed the boy's hand and patted it repeatedly. Charles looked like he wanted to pull it away. "What have you done, Chadbourn?" Sylvia spat over her shoulder. "He may never be normal. He may never walk. He may—"

Will saw stark alarm on the boy's face. "Nonsense, Sylvia, it's a clean cut. He will heal up fine." He glanced at Catherine, who eyed the parlor door. He didn't want her to bolt. They needed to talk.

"Randy says I may get an excellent scar," Charles, relieved, put in with pride.

"Randy? We don't associate with any 'Randy.' Those horrid boys did this, didn't they? Emery was right to run them off. You will call the magistrate, Chadbourn. I insist on it." She continued to chafe Charles's hand, while the boy tried in vain to tug away.

"No, Mama," Charles insisted. "Randy didn't do anything. I climbed up the fence to watch Freddy and slipped. It was my fault, but Randy says he slips all the time, and I just need practice."

"Randy says? Randy says? What does he have to say about it? That lot at Songbird Cottage are not received, Charles. You will not go near them again. You will keep yourself to the schoolroom with dear Franklin." She hiccupped a sob. "We must send to London for a physician."

"You might want a physician or surgeon to look at it," Catherine said quietly to Will. "There is an excellent medical practitioner in Wheatton. I doubt he will do more than I, however. Until then, I recommend you keep it clean. Reapply honey when you change the bandages tomorrow."

"You let this woman touch my son? With *honey*? We will send for Wetherby, of course. He will come from London posthaste, but this honey will *horrify* him." Sylvia rose to glare at Catherine. "She's from Songbird Cottage, isn't she? One of them?" She didn't wait for an answer. She lifted her chin and addressed Catherine directly.

"Get you gone. Stay away, and keep your sons away from mine," Sylvia spat.

Catherine drew herself to her full height and returned Sylvia's haughty look with one of her own. "I will gladly leave, and I will make sure *my brothers* know they aren't welcome here, as I had intended when I came." She turned to Charles, neatly giving Sylvia the cut direct, her slight bow acknowledging the boy's title, for his mother's sake. The smile she gave him looked genuine, but strained. "I hope this scratch doesn't trouble you unduly, Your Grace. Don't let it keep you from enjoying the out of doors. My lord," she said, with a nod at Chadbourn. She, and took her long-limbed stride to the door.

"Miss Wheatly, wait!" She didn't.

~

BLASTED SNOOTY ARISTOCRATS. Catherine rounded the hall into Eversham's vaulted and, in Catherine's opinion, over-decorated, foyer. *I'll be damned if I skulk out the tradesmen's door like a charwoman.* She refused to recall the last time she had come to this door. Her half-boots pounded on the floor mosaics and echoed off the gilt cherubs on the molding. She could hear the earl call for her to stop. If he thought he could detain her, he was as big a fool as his ninnyhammer sister.

She reached the front door before he caught up with her. "Please don't go," he said breathlessly, putting out a hand.

She jerked her arm up so he couldn't touch her.

"Do you plan to throw me in the dirt?" she demanded, when she spun on him.

"What? No. I want to talk to you about Charles."

His sister treats me like dirt, and he wants to talk about the duke? She scowled at him.

"I apologize for my sister. She is in a fragile state, and I'm afraid the sight of the bandages sent her wits begging."

"I doubt it. From the looks of the duchess's pupils, an excess of laudanum scrambled those wits long ago."

The pain in Chadbourn's eyes caught her. *He must genuinely love the woman.* He bit his lower lip; Catherine found herself captivated by the sight.

"My sister was not well served in her marriage," he said hesitantly.

"The generosity of spirit she had as a girl disappeared." He looked directly at Catherine. "I can't seem to bring it back."

For a moment, he looked as if he meant to ask Catherine for help, as if she could heal the duchess's hurts, but he quickly came to his senses. "I'm sorry. I have no right to burden you with my problems."

She nodded firmly. "You wanted to talk about the young duke?"

He asked her briefly about wound care. He obviously knew more about it than he let on, but he asked, and she repeated what she had already told him.

"Try not to let that society doctor treat him," she added. "He will want to bleed the boy. That's their answer to everything."

The earl nodded. "I didn't plan to allow it. When do you think he'll be able to meet with the boys again?"

The question startled her.

"You have been here two months, and will be here two more. You must see that the breach between Songbird and Eversham runs deep. Let it rest."

"I will not. Charles needs boys his age. His cousins—I'm right that they are his cousins, am I not?"

She couldn't deny it. She nodded.

"His cousins can give him not just companionship, but the confidence he desperately needs. You have no idea how pleased I am he attempted to climb a fence, even if it didn't end well. He has had no chance to be a normal boy. I want that for him, and I'll have it."

He means it. This interfering earl is going to storm into our lives, upset Papa more than his bloody damned lordship can imagine, and then leave.

"Very well, my lord," she said. "Your nephew is welcome to visit Songbird Cottage whenever you like. However, under no circumstances will I, or my brothers, step foot here again."

Storm clouds again. "You should be welcome here," he ground out.

"We aren't—" *The last time I came, only Papa's illness and desperation for his sake brought me. The duke set two footmen to toss me out the tradesmen's door.* "—And obviously, that hasn't changed. I'll bid you good day."

The earl put a hand on Catherine's arm to hold her in place; she didn't expect it. In her agitation, she jumped, and he dropped his hand as if it burnt.

The earl's coffee-colored eyes bore into hers. "I didn't mean to frighten you. I saw the look on your face."

"My face?"

"Out there, by the paddock, when I asked you in. For a moment, you were afraid."

She didn't deny it.

"What did Emery do to you? Did he force you?"

The sting of her slap echoed through the house. "What do you take me for?"

He rubbed his cheek. "I take you for an innocent who has been badly treated by this house, damn it!"

Too angry to speak, Catherine struggled to catch her breath. She felt heat rise up from between her breasts to inflame her cheeks.

Chadbourn ran a hand through his unruly hair. "I'm making a muddle of this. I apologize if my concern gave offense."

"Accepted. May I go?"

"Of course you may. Stop acting like I'm coercing you."

He wasn't. Not really. Catherine urged herself to stop acting out a Cheltenham tragedy over it.

The earl heaved a great sigh. "Stay away if you wish. What I'm trying to do is ask for your help. With your permission, Charles and I will call on you when he feels better." His brown eyes pleaded for understanding.

"Very well, my lord. I wish you well convincing the boy's mother." She spun on her heel and left.

A FEW DAYS LATER, Catherine watched the three boys make their way toward the orchard, Freddy and Randy skipping about, the young duke stiff and uncertain, but determined. Bertha, the dog, scampered around them. November had just passed into December, but the chill was slight.

After an awkward visit of several uncomfortable minutes, Chadbourn had enticed the boys with a suggestion they reenact some lurid episode of the Wars of the Roses. Even the young duke seemed eager to defend Lancaster or York. She wasn't sure which.

"That was neatly done, if I do say so." The earl's rich baritone vibrated through her. He sounded smug.

"Rather! My brothers are pleased to be loosed from their studies."

"So is Charles, not that I think his studies are getting him far. His tutor is worthless."

At least he has one, she thought as she turned to find the earl smiling at her.

"Did you come here today merely to disrupt the peace of our orchard with Lancastrian armies?" she asked.

"No, no. I came to thank you for giving me Squire Archer's direction. I admit, it gave me an excuse to bring Charles, though. I told you he needs to meet boys his age."

"The duchess allowed it?"

"The duchess doesn't know." If he felt any guilt for hiding it from his sister, he hid it well.

"His Grace is certainly polite."

The earl groaned. "Etiquette is well enough. Your brothers certainly know how to behave. Charles uses good manners as a shield to hide behind."

Catherine looked at the man next to her. His title and fashionable dress marked him as someone comfortable in the halls of power and fashionable drawing rooms, and still, he worried about a boy with an excess of manners. She could see more when she looked closely. He had the sun-darkened skin, disordered hair, and broad shoulders of a man at ease in the out of doors. An insight came to her.

"You want that for your nephew," she said. She met his eyes.

"Want what?"

"Comfort in the out of doors."

"More than comfort. Passion for the land, for the fields and woodlots, for the people. The country is our true home."

Catherine felt her mouth widen into a smile and knew it reached her eyes. She saw the echo in his.

~

PASSION. *This woman shares it. I can see it in her eyes.*

"Shall we go to the house?" He smiled at her. He stood well over six feet, so, of course, he had to look down, but not as far as he might. Catherine came up to his shoulder. *She would fit there nicely*, he thought with a private smile.

She looked sideways at him as they reached the door. "So, what do you wish to discuss? Wheat yields or milk production?"

Blatant change of subject. He couldn't be irritated with this brilliant woman. "Wool, Miss Wheatly. What am I going to do with all those blasted sheep? The late duke apparently believed that if a small herd made a profit, quadrupling it would make four times as much. The pasture land can't support them, and thanks to his steward's stupidity, we can't afford to feed them over the winter, either."

The woman launched into a recital of the ratio of sheep to meadow, "Though we haven't the land to keep sheep ourselves," and provided several shrewd ideas about ways to dispose of the blighters before winter took full hold. Will listened with half an ear, tucking away the thoughts to share with Archer.

He had far more interest in the color talk of husbandry brought to Catherine's cheeks. He had a sudden vision of seeing that face over breakfast every morning while they went over the business of their own estate. The thought stunned him.

"What is it, my lord?" Catherine asked, watching him closely. "You look as if you've had a fright."

"Not a fright, merely an unexpected thought," he replied. *One much too soon to talk about.* "It's nothing." He pushed the thought of Catherine at his table to the back of his mind. He needed to marshal all his attention for the conversation he wanted to have with Lord Arthur.

~

HER FATHER TURNED SO dark with rage, Catherine feared for his heart.

"We do well enough, damn you. We don't need Eversham's charity. Not now, not after everything," the old man raged.

Chadbourn had bungled in as she feared, but what he laid out had been generous and well intended. *Papa's old hurts are in the way of his reason.*

"Think, man," Chadbourn soothed. "The boys deserve an education at least. They are a duke's grandsons. Don't tell me they aren't."

Papa's chin quivered with pent-up emotion. "I won't deny that, but that doesn't make it the Earl of Chadbourn's business."

"As long as the duke is my ward, it does. The estate has an obligation, and I intend to see it met. The least owed is to educate them as gentlemen and prepare them for professions."

"Randy doesn't want a profession," Catherine cut in. "He will be content to be a farmer."

"Be that as it may, he can be an educated farmer, just as I am, title or not. What of Freddy? Horse mad and eager for glory. The cavalry—"

"You want to send my boy off to war?" Papa shouted. Catherine felt sick at thought. Yet, she had to admit to herself, she feared Freddy would take the king's shilling just to get away from farming. School and an officer's colors would be better.

"No, no. That would be up to Freddy. For now, schooling. Charles is bound for Eton next year, and having friends with him would ease his way."

"Not that damned place. My father condemned me there."

Chadbourn smiled broadly, taking Catherine off guard. "Harrow it is," he said. "Much better. My own school. It can be just as harsh, but friends make it bearable. The boys would be together."

Papa looked like steam gathered for another explosion. "Nothing need be decided today," Catherine soothed. "Perhaps Mrs. MacLeish has that tea ready." As if on cue, the woman herself knocked and entered with a tray of tea and biscuits.

"Oh look, Papa. She made your favorite butter biscuits." Catherine smiled at the woman who had fed her family since Catherine was a tot. Mrs. MacLeish gave her a cheeky wink. "Thank you," Catherine whispered.

Tea and sweets soothed ruffled feathers, but settled nothing. An uncomfortable hour later, she walked the earl out.

"Give him time to get used to the idea. He's been estranged for so long."

The earl took her hand, but instead of bowing over it, he held it firmly and searched her face.

"What breach keeps him from accepting the support any well-managed estate would give?" His eyes held nothing but sympathy and concern.

She couldn't deny him.

"I don't entirely know. I was just twelve years old. My mother and I had been living with an aunt in Scotland. Papa brought us back to Wheatton to see her father, who was vicar here, before he died. The old duke, his father, disowned him when he married my mother, but could do nothing about Songbird Cottage. Papa's mother left it to him. I think the old man resented that."

He looked as if he meant to ask more; she prayed he didn't. *What am I to say? No, my mother wasn't married when I was born? No, Lord Arthur isn't my natural father?*

Before he could, three boys came raging from the woods.

"The owl, Cath! We saw him," Randy called.

Once sufficient amazement over the sighting had been expressed, Chadbourn helped the young duke into their phaeton. He bowed over Catherine's hand and took his leave, but his eyes never lost their sympathetic look. It was almost enough to give a woman hope. *Damn the man.*

Catherine turned from the sight. *The duchess will not like this day's activity*, she thought.

6

"But he came in smelling of cow, Chadbourn! And not for the first time. I told Franklin to burn his clothing, burn it! You must allow Franklin to birch him." Sylvia sat upright, but her hands shook, and her pupils looked large in her rheumy eyes.

"I will not!"

"Emery would have," she whined. "He would demand it."

"Emery was a jackass, and I am not Emery, for which, sister, you should be thankful." Will clenched his hands into fists to keep from wrapping them around the scrawny neck of the tutor who held his nephew by the jacket, held him so high, the boy's feet almost lifted from the floor. Charles held his face in a brave show of courage, but his eyes pleaded with Chadbourn.

"Unhand His Grace this instant," Will shouted. "You will not birch him today or any other day. Has this happened before?"

"Only when necessary," Franklin said, chin up, eyes on Sylvia. "Boys require discipline." He gave Charles a shake as he pushed the lad away.

Will put an arm around the boy's shoulder. He could feel tension vibrating through the young body, but Charles held himself upright.

"From the state of his math knowledge, I suspect he has had more 'discipline' than learning from you."

"One cannot teach what he will not learn, my lord." Franklin made the title sound like an insult. "I only follow His Grace'sthat is the late duke's—wishes," the man sniveled.

"You finally got one thing right. His Grace's father is the *late* duke. I will not have my nephew beaten, and certainly not over a trivial offense."

"Trivial?" Sylvia cried, bringing a look of satisfaction to the tutor. "He snuck away from his tutor. He went *there*, Chadbourn."

Will ignored her. He looked Franklin up and down. "You're dismissed," he said as calmly as he could manage.

"Fired?" The tutor shook with outrage. "For following His Grace's orders?"

"For failing to follow mine, and for failing to teach this boy a blasted thing. Go pack your things." When Franklin glanced frantically at Sylvia and looked as if he would argue, Will held up a hand. "Pack your things without a word, and I'll allow the duchess to provide you with a character reference. Otherwise, I will toss you bodily from the house without it."

Sylvia cowered beneath Will's tone, and wept.

"He went there, Chadbourn. Emery forbade it. We do not go there."

"He went with me yesterday, and he will have my permission to go again," Will said. He watched the tutor wrap his dignity around him and leave.

Sylvia began to hiccup, tiny sobs emanating from her.

Will turned to Charles and smiled into the boy's pale face. "You do look rather a mess, my boy. You didn't tell me you went back and left the schoolroom without permission."

"Sorry, Uncle Will. Fred and Randy sent a message up with John Footman, and I had to meet them. I had to."

"Your mother is right about one thing. This suit is ruined. Do you own clothes that aren't silk, something suitable for playing?"

"No, sir."

Of course not. "We'll see to it. For now, remove those clothes and have them laundered for the poor box. For leaving without permission, I want you to spend the rest of the day writing out your multiplication tables. Understood?"

Charles grimaced. "Yes, Uncle Will."

The boy left, and Will turned to his sister, determined to get to the bottom of the animosity with Songbird Cottage, but she had already slipped into a drug-induced sleep.

~

"You've been busy. I rather think you didn't need my help." The Marquess of Glenaire, who had arrived just as Will saw the tutor on his way, sat at his leisure over port.

Thank God he came today before I strangled the rotter and did the same to Stowe, Will thought. The man's hostile glares put him in mind to turn off the butler next. *I would if he weren't so blasted old. Better to pension him off, and soon.*

"Oh, but I do," he said. "Besides, you'll enliven the winter holidays."

White-blond eyebrows shot up over ice-blue eyes. "I'm hardly one for the sentiments of the season."

"Even your hidebound dignity improves the mood of this place, Richard. It is driving me to drink." He downed another glass, while he poured out his woes to his best friend in the world. "What can you add?" he asked when he his tale wound down.

"Not much. Lord Arthur is, as you surmised, the second son of the seventh duke of Murnane. By reputation, he presented a mild-mannered contrast to his rakehell older brother, when the two came down from university. Lord Arthur actually finished a degree and took a first. He went about during the Season for a few years, sowed a few wild oats—damned few—courted a few chits unenthusiastically, and avoided house parties. He shunned society entirely after his marriage. He supports himself on a meager income from his books."

"That, and a well-run farm. What about his marriage?"

"He wed Miss Mary Harlow, daughter of the Wheatton vicar, in 1801. Their son, Frederick, was born less than a year, but more than nine months, later."

"Catherine?"

Glenaire's sardonic look at Will's use of her given name spoke volumes, but the marquess didn't comment on it. "About Miss Wheatly, if that is her name, I could find little. Her mother departed Wheatton abruptly late in 1788, and came to live with an aunt in a remote village in Scotland, with an infant, soon after. Of marriage or a father, we found no trace. I have people looking into it, but, if there is no paper, they are reduced to listening at keyholes."

"Call them off."

The eyebrows rose.

"We can assume the obvious. No point in causing Catherine embarrassment or upsetting Lord Arthur any further. The man is fiercely protective of her." Will watched the deep purple liquid swirl around in his glass. "It might help to know, however," he murmured.

"To what purpose?" Glenaire asked, knowing eyes boring into him.

Before I take her to wed. He couldn't say the words out loud. Not until he was certain enough of his own feelings to put them to the test. "Something isn't right," he said instead. "Nothing you've said accounts for the animosity. Emery put the fear of God into Sylvia. She seems to believe Catherine—Miss Wheatly—was Emery's mistress."

"Perhaps she was."

"No!"

Glenaire waited with exquisite patience.

"I would bet Chadbourn Park on it. If Emery took Catherine, it wasn't voluntarily. It might account for his determination to keep Charles and Sylvia away, though I just can't see it. What of Songbird Cottage?"

Glenaire leaned forward and put both elbows on the table, cupping his glass. "Songbird Cottage and its acres belong outright to

Lord Arthur, left to him by his mother from her settlements. Neither the seventh nor eighth duke had any claim to it."

Will nodded. "Catherine said as much. She said his father resented it."

"Some men would dislike loss of control."

"Isn't that the point of settlements, protecting something for the woman and her children?"

"True, but some begrudge it. Perhaps, the old duke expected it to come directly to him upon marriage. Perhaps Emery felt the same. Is it a nice piece of land?"

"Not large, but tidy and productive. The best."

"There you have it."

"Maybe. There has to be more, and I'm going to find it, for those boys' sake if nothing else. They are a duke's grandsons. The estate owes them better. A gentleman's education, at least."

Long minutes passed. Glenaire watched Will. Will stared at his port until he finally sat back and let a grim smile show. "I think it's time Lord Arthur visits his childhood home."

"From what you have said, he won't come."

"Catherine will persuade him, if only for her brothers' wellbeing. I have her support for that, at least. She hasn't said it, but I know it's there. She'll persuade him."

He counted on it.

7

"Brilliant!" Randy shouted.

He ran up the hill to greet his new friend. Charles walked down the lane herding three sheep, his uncle close behind. The boys had managed to contrive reasons to visit every other day, and now, the young duke had been dragooned into the animal nativity.

"I herded them myself," Charles crowed. "I told Uncle Will we needed sheep, and he said they were mine to give, but I wasn't to ask Mr. Archer to bring them. I had to figure out how to get them here."

"Dead perfect, Charles!" Freddy exclaimed. "These will fill out the nativity nicely. How did you learn to herd?"

Catherine looked at the earl's amused brown eyes. "Your Grace" seemed to have fled sometime in the last week.

"I found a book in the library, *A Guide for Young Shepherds*. It described how to herd them, and a whole lot more besides. Book was exactly right: it's easy. Will these do, then?"

Randy hugged one sheep around the neck and scratched the ears of another. "Are they ours to keep?"

"Certainly," Charles said regally. "I'm giving them to you."

"Can we, Cath? We don't have to give them back after Christmas, do we?"

She looked at Chadbourn for enlightenment, but his amused expression made it clear she was on her own.

"Do you think we have enough feed for winter?" she asked even though she knew the answer perfectly well.

Randy gave it some thought. "Yes, we do. We stocked more than we needed, in case. I guess it was in case we got three sheep! We'll need that book, though."

"Who will be the shepherd?" Freddy asked. "For the nativity, that is. Do you think we could borrow Lady Guinevere?"

"You could, but she's too big," Charles said. "Oh, I forgot to tell you. I fed her a carrot yesterday without help." He grinned at the boys. "She's to be my mount, as soon as we become friends," he confided.

"Excellent, Charles. I told you it wasn't hard," Randy said. The duke beamed proudly.

The three, and their woolly friends, wandered off to the barn, arguing about what animal might stand for a shepherd. Randy argued correctly that Bertha, who was a sheepdog, would be the logical choice. "But she's going to be Mother Mary. If we make her a shepherd, where will we be?" Freddy insisted, lobbying for the loan of a horse.

When the barn door closed, Chadbourn and Catherine convulsed in laughter.

"Oh, my lord," Catherine laughed, tears rolling down her cheeks. "However am I going to keep from laughing on Christmas morning? I will disgrace myself during services."

"Will."

"I beg your pardon?"

"My name is William. Two people who laugh so hard together certainly ought to make use of given names, Catherine." His expression held a challenge.

She looked to the house, as if she could hear her father's fervent admonition about trusting titled blackguards, from the yard.

"Say it. Say my name."

"Will," she whispered. She felt a blush heat her cheeks. "For this moment. For the laughter, but not—"

"—not when I talk with your father? Have you convinced him I'm right about your brothers?"

She shook her head, a sly smile appearing only briefly. "Not quite. I'm wearing him down, though."

When he took her hand, she let him. When he drew it toward his lips rather than bowing over her fingers, she let him. When he cupped her cheek and leaned in to kiss her, she almost let him.

"Unhand my daughter, you damned rakehell!" Papa stood in the doorway in full outrage. She felt bereft when his warmth pulled away.

"Ah, Lord Arthur, just the person I came to see."

Papa looked skeptical, but he held the door. "Come in, then, and get at it." He glared at Catherine.

She watched the door close behind the two men. It was the third such visit. She suspected her father had come to enjoy sparring with the earl, and was holding out just for the fun of it.

The boys would be in school the following fall. The thought dampened her spirits. The earl would leave sooner. That thought depressed them thoroughly. One attempted kiss notwithstanding, the bastard daughter of a country scholar did not aspire to be Countess of Chadbourn.

"WILL THIS DO?" the earl—she would not let herself think of him as Will—called from the top of the tree. He waved a large sprig of mistletoe triumphantly.

"It certainly will. Now, come down before you break your neck," Catherine said in her best older-sister voice. He had visited her father twice more. The second time, he brought his friend, the marquess, who frightened both of her brothers into awed silence, no small feat. The elegant and reserved marquess confirmed Catherine's belief that the earl's world lay far outside of her experience or ambition.

The marquess also leant a firm hand and logic to the earl's persuasion of her father, however. Papa, she thought, was poised on the brink of capitulating.

When Chadbourn heard they were going to gather greens to decorate Songbird, there was nothing for it but to invite the young duke along. His uncle had to accompany him, of course. The marquess wisely declined. Her father snorted about nonsense, but didn't forbid it.

"Isn't he grand, Cath?" Randy exclaimed. "He climbed up there like he does it every day, not like some stuck-up earl." He did, at that. She tried to imagine the Marquess of Glenaire at the top of the tree and failed miserably.

The not-so-stuck-up earl grinned down at her. "Catch!" he shouted, and she scrambled to obey. He climbed down with the same grace and alacrity with which he climbed up. Catherine watched in rapt fascination, mistletoe clutched to her breast.

"Cath won't usually let us get the mistletoe. We make do with holly," Freddy told Charles. At least the earl's efforts kept her brothers from breaking their foolish necks.

Will leapt down from the lowest branch, landing on his feet, with laughter in his eyes. "Mistletoe is the best part, Freddy," he said. "Let me demonstrate." He moved toward Catherine, a predatory look taking the place of laughter in his expression.

Catherine took a step back, still clutching the mistletoe. She tried to control panic. *Don't be a ninnyhammer. What can he do in front of the boys?*

When Will pulled her hands forward and took a sprig, she couldn't take her eyes from his. "When a lady finds herself under mistletoe," he told the boys without looking away from Catherine, "she must pay the forfeit." He leaned in, and her eyes focused on his lips, his fine, chiseled lips. Her mouth parted in amazement just as he closed the distance between them. He took her lower lip in his gently, before moving over her mouth in a caress that took her breath. Before she could disgrace herself by clutching his neck and drawing him closer, he pulled back and smiled knowingly.

"That, my boys, is how it's done," he said hoarsely, without taking his eyes from her face.

"Take the mistletoe back," Freddy crowed, while Randy made retching noises. The duke looked from one of his friends to the other and joined in the mockery.

"Oh, very well," Chadbourn said. "You may use this option, too." He leaned in and kissed her cheek quickly. Only then, did Catherine realize his arm on her waist steadied her. If he hadn't held her, her knees might have buckled.

He looked at her, as if to confirm she could stand, and turned briskly.

"Let's get these greens to the house," he said, and organized the boys for the trek back to the kitchen. When they got there and unloaded greenery all over Mrs. MacLeish's worktable, Will announced he would pay his respects to Lord Arthur.

Catherine bolted to her room before he could ask her to join him and have a private moment along the way.

Two hours later, she stood in her father's study in shock. Not only had Lord Arthur agreed to the boy's schooling, he had agreed to come to Eversham Hall to discuss arrangements.

"Boy's right. I may as well face it sooner rather than later."

He would face his childhood home. And Catherine? She would face dinner with a hostile duchess, a toplofty marquess, and an earl who made mush of her senses and left her unable to think. *Damn it, anyway*. She couldn't wait.

FOR THE MOST PART, it went well, Will thought later. Sylvia, fortified by two weeks of dinners with the marquess, and mindful of Will's orders to be welcoming, had behaved. It didn't hurt that her new lady's maid had been watering her 'tonic,' gradually decreasing the drug's effect. Will determined to give the woman a bonus.

The evening began well. Randy and Freddy, scrubbed and dressed in their church clothes, followed a footman to the nursery floor, where Charles had planned more War of the Roses. Will hoped they confined themselves to the army of toy soldiers he had liberated from the attic, in a box labeled "Master Arthur." No crashes, screams, or other catastrophes indicated otherwise.

Catherine made proper curtsey to the marquess and the duchess. The dress she wore, a lovely green muslin, flattered her curves and brought out the gold in her auburn hair. She would look spectacular in green watered silk. Will would see to it. He no longer had any doubts that Catherine would be his countess, her origins and Sylvia's nerves be damned.

Lord Arthur worried him at first. Stowe had stiffened showing him in, but Lord Arthur managed a sardonic twinkle. "It has been many years, Stowe. The prodigal has returned." He bowed to Sylvia, who seemed utterly bemused to discover her uncomfortable neighbor was, in fact, her brother-in-law. That she didn't know Will put down to Emery's pure negligence, if not spite. Sylvia eyed Catherine speculatively, but said nothing. *God be praised.*

"Is it as you remember, Papa?" Catherine asked.

"Oh, yes," the old man said. "You've made few changes, Your Grace." He looked at Sylvia sympathetically. Will suspected the old man must guess what it had been like for her, living with his father and brother. "Perhaps now ..." Lord Arthur's voice trailed away while his eyes scanned the gilt and ornate foyer.

Glenaire put his diplomatic and social polish to use, keeping the conversation flowing over dinner. When politics failed, literature worked. When the social season proved no interest to the company, Glenaire spoke of education. He and Will told stories of their boyhood at Harrow, and their successes, along with their friends Jamie Heyworth and Andrew Mallet, in keeping the worst of the bullying at bay. Lord Arthur seemed to find that reassuring. Catherine provided no input at all.

"Heyworth—a baron, if I recall correctly," Lord Arthur said.

"His father, yes. But the son is nothing like the father," Will told him.

"Thank goodness," Glenaire said. "Jamie lives on half-pay since Waterloo, but he served in the cavalry like Will for seven years, by all accounts, with distinction."

"You were in the army?" Catherine asked, suddenly alert. She searched him, as if assessing damage.

"Neither as long, nor as well, as Jamie," Will answered. "I sold out three years ago to take over for my father. He died six months after I came home."

"Did you miss it?"

"The mud and the horror of it? No. But I should have been in Belgium."

"Nonsense, Chadbourn," Glenaire said. "Andrew and Jamie were enough of a contribution to the wretched Corsican."

"Were they wounded?" Catherine asked. The compassion in her expression warmed Will's heart.

"Andrew was badly damaged," Glenaire told her. "He has gone home to Cambridge to heal. Jamie came through unscathed."

"In body, perhaps. Not all wounds are visible," Will said sadly. He caught his friend's eye. When he looked away, he found Catherine looking at him speculatively. Could he tell her about war? Most men would not; most women wouldn't want to hear. Somehow, he thought this woman strong enough to bear whatever burdens he chose to share.

Glenaire skillfully moved the conversation to the weather, always a safe choice. The impact of weather on agriculture drew knowledgeable comments from Catherine. A brief discussion about her father's work put color in her cheeks. She understood the publishing business as well as she knew wheat cultivation. *She'll succeed at whatever she tries*, Will thought proudly.

When Sylvia rose, the panic on Catherine's face brought Will to his feet. "We needn't be formal among family, gentlemen. I suggest we join the ladies for after-dinner refreshment." *And buffer Catherine from Sylvia's company.*

Conversation in the withdrawing room did not go as well. Sylvia's control started to slip, and something in the room bothered Lord Arthur.

"You were right, Chadbourn. Sometimes, a man has to face his demons," the old man said. "But if this room were mine, I would strip it of its furnishings and change it completely."

Catherine looked suddenly wary. She put a hand on her father's arm. Lord Arthur, however, appeared lost in his own thoughts. "This is where I told m'father I planned to wed my Mary."

Stunned silence greeted that announcement.

"He disapproved," Will said, and immediately regretted it, when Lord Arthur went on as if he hadn't heard.

"Beat me over the head." He pointed to a finely carved side chair next to the folded card table. "There used to be two of those. He broke one over my shoulder. Dislocated it. I never saw him again."

Lord Arthur looked around at the company and blinked. "I am sorry, Your Grace," he said to Sylvia, who had gone pale as a ghost. "Old history."

"Chadbourn, I... I feel poorly. I need to lie down," the duchess said, rising unsteadily to her feet. Will wondered, fleetingly, what ghost Lord Arthur's description of violence had resurrected, but he took her elbow to assist her.

He stopped and addressed Lord Arthur. They had come this far; he couldn't let it drop.

"Why? What did he have against your lady?" he asked.

Perhaps it was his use of "lady" to describe Mary, but Lord Arthur seemed to stand a bit straighter. "Believed the disgrace would 'taint' the family, as if we didn't have worse blots on our family escutcheon, as if my Mary weren't a treasure that would enrich any family."

Will opened his mouth to ask more, but Sylvia sagged against him.

"Come, girl, we'd best leave," Lord Arthur said to Catherine. "I hope you feel better, Your Grace. I'm sorry I upset your evening." Lord Arthur bowed correctly, but left the room without pausing.

Catherine looked at Will, perplexity and sorı expression.

"We'll talk later," he said.

~

CATHERINE DESPERATELY WISHED THAT "LATER" meant in a year or two. She wished, at least, that Will would give her a week to think about his sister's distress, to recover from her father's revelation, and to steel herself against the perilous attraction she felt every time he came close. He gave her no such time.

The big bay trotted down the lane, raising dust and Freddy's hopes. For weeks now, the earl had arrived by phaeton with Charles. Today, he came alone.

"Where can we talk?" he asked without preamble, while Freddy happily led Mercury to the meadow for "a gentle walk."

"Alone?" she asked. She shouldn't be alone with him. She couldn't.

"Catherine, I won't hurt you. I won't—" He broke off with a curse and led her to the tool storage closet in the barn.

She tripped along next to him, and her thoughts raced.

He closed the door and pulled her into a fierce kiss, before putting a hand on each arm and setting her carefully away.

Trapped between a desire to slap his face and a sharper desire to throw herself into his arms, Catherine crossed her arms around her waist, as if to protect herself.

Will ran a hand through his hair. "I'm sorry. That probably doesn't help my cause, but I thought of nothing else last night." He took a steadying breath.

"I won't be your mistress," Catherine burst out, unable to hold the thought in.

"What? Of course not! What do you take me for?"

"I take you for an earl who has family and friends among the highest ranks in England, who knows full well the place of a baseborn daughter of a country squire. But, Will, I can't do it." *She searched his eyes, begging silently for understanding.*

"Aren't you getting ahead of me? What I need first is a friend, a friend and a partner."

"What do you mean?"

"I carried on alone for months, Catherine. My father died, and Chadbourn Park fell to me. He left it in good condition, but the responsibility weighed on me. Before I met you, I had no idea how lonely I had become."

She could formulate no reply to that.

"I came here to find the land abused, disasters everywhere, and, well, you've met Sylvia and know my worries for Charles. Before I met you, I was at my wits end."

"You're managing well. What did I do?"

"You found me Archer, for one, and a market for the excess of blasted sheep. You rescued Charles."

"I?"

He grinned ruefully. "Perhaps your brothers rescued Charles." He sobered quickly. "You have no idea how I feared for him. His father left him so nervous and afraid, that everything I said made him cringe. Freddy and Randy have been a blessing."

She nodded. "Animals that have been beaten or abused are like that. Love and attention usually works, but not always. You give him that."

"Friendship helps. It helped him. I need it, too. I think my sister does, also."

"She won't welcome me."

"She did well, at first, last night."

"Until my father's story upset her."

"I don't think he meant to do that."

"No, and I don't believe his story was the main problem," Catherine mused. "I've been thinking about her."

"What do you mean?"

"There was an elderly man in the village, the shopkeeper's uncle. He had been in His Majesty's Navy for many years. He came to live here, because he could no longer support himself. The me he was one of three survivors of a ship that took a direct powder room. It blew up around him. Once he was back on la. sent him running. Loud noises of any kind made him shake .d weep. He would hide in shame."

"He relived the memory over and over. I saw men like that in the army," Will mused.

Catherine decided to take a chance. "It isn't my business, Will, but did your sister experience violence at the hands of Papa's father?"

His face looked bleak. "Perhaps. At her husband's hands, without any doubt, although she won't talk about it."

"I think Papa's story triggered her own memories. I suspect she uses the tonic to deaden them. Give her time."

"I have given her time. She needs to be pushed out of her stupor. Last night helped."

"Helped? She almost collapsed."

He shook his head. "She can't hide, any more than your father can."

"What do you suggest?"

"Come again, this time for longer. Stay one night. Christmas Eve. The boys will love it, and it may give your father time to get his stories out. He needs to. Sylvia needs to, also."

She thought about it. "It might work, at least for Papa. Not the twenty-fourth, though. Papa takes us to Christmas Vespers, and then we eat cakes and tell stories. The boys will expect it."

The longing in Will's face struck her to the heart. *How long has it been since he had family intimacy?*

"I won't interfere," he said sadly. "Come the day and night before, and share some of your stories with us. Please."

She couldn't deny him. "I'll try to convince Papa. He may be ready to come again. He has had many good years here to strengthen him."

"And Sylvia does not?"

She shook her head. "Too soon, I think."

"Let's make a start, at least. I can face the thing with a partner," he told her.

"Partner?"

"A partner makes many things more bearable. They can make the impossible possible." He took her hand.

"I'll bring Papa for a visit, if you wish," she agreed.

"Cath? Cath? Come and see how the piglet looks in Freddy's old baby bonnet," Randy called from outside.

Catherine clamped a hand over her mouth to suppress a laugh at the picture Randy's words created. Will's laughing eyes made her drop her hand to smile back. Before she could think, he dared a quick kiss, thrust her deeper into shadows, and stepped out. "I am looking for her, too, Randy. "Let's try behind the house."

~

WILL WISHED DESPERATELY that Catherine stood at his side two days later, when Sylvia soaked his neck-cloth and sobbed all over his jacket. Three boys looked on with wide eyes and troubled expressions.

"The boys meant no harm," he murmured. *What can I say to heal this madness?*

"Truly, we didn't, Mama," Charles said. Hands still holding pine branches hung at his side. "I invited Randy and Freddy to help make the hall look festive."

Sylvia's muffled reply was unintelligible. The boy continued desperately, "It's just that Songbird Cottage looks ever so festive, and we never do anything..." He groped for a word. "Fun. We never laugh," he finished, anguish in his voice.

Sylvia lifted her head and took a look at her son. "But, Charles, we're in mourning."

Charles raised a defiant, if trembling, chin. "We've been in mourning my whole life."

She gasped, and Will braced for another outburst. What she said next surprised him.

"We have, haven't we? Ten years of mourning. Never any joy. No smiles over dinner. No guests. Never any holiday greens. No

Christmas pudding. No Twelfth Night revels, not here, not with family. No joy. Even Boxing Day felt like a court ceremony, and no one ever told me the rules." She gave a little hiccup and put her head on Will's shoulder. "I always got them wrong."

He hugged her close.

"Oh, Will, do you remember how Father used to make the household laugh on Boxing Day?" she asked.

"I remember. I didn't think you did. Do you remember how Mother organized Twelfth Night revels?"

Sylvia cried again, but with less desperation. To Will, it felt like the soul-shaking cry of mourning. She mourned, he suspected, the loss of youth, family, and joy, not her husband.

He gathered her close and spoke to the boys over her shoulder.

"You're right to bring joy to this house, Charles, but perhaps the grand foyer is not the place to start." *It will take more than the boys' efforts at decoration to make this monstrosity feel human.* "I suggest you start with the nursery."

Charles's face fell, but he complied. He picked up one pile of branches. "Come up with me, Randy and Freddy. At least upstairs, no one will interrupt us."

"Wait, boys," Will said. "You could also decorate the family parlor. Celebrations belong best with family, no?"

"Famous, Charles! We'll all be there, won't we, my lord?" Randy looked at Will hopefully.

"You certainly will. We'll all be together tomorrow night." *I have no idea how I'll make sure joy outweighs grief, but I'm damn well going to try.* "There will be gifts," he said with a wink.

"Excellent notion!" Charles exclaimed.

"Come on, Charles. A parlor will be easier to do, anyway," Freddy suggested. "We were going to need a big ladder for this one, and that Stowe liked to have apoplexy when we brought in the greens." He looked around the cavernous foyer. "It would be a good place for the nativity pageant, though."

"Don't even think about it," Will called over Sylvia's shoulder at the retreating boys.

In the boys' absence, Sylvia's quiet weeping echoed off the walls. "Come, dear one, let's go upstairs." He kept an arm around his sister's shoulders while he led her to the stairs. "Were the decorations so terrible?"

"They aren't terrible at all," she said, her voice thick with tears. "It reminded me of Chadbourn Park. Emery never allowed it. He never allowed us to celebrate."

"I thought Emery liked his pleasures."

"He spent the weeks at house parties, but he left orders. Once, I put up holly in the parlor and took it down before he returned."

"Good for you."

"Stowe told him. Emery beat me and turned off the two servants who helped. I never did it again. He hated me." He felt a tremor go through her body and wished his late brother-in-law to one of the lower rungs of Hell. *At least she finally said the words*, he thought.

When they reached her room, Will took her face in his hands. "Someday, Sister, when you are ready, you will tell me everything, and I will tell you again how very sorry I am that I didn't protect you from that man."

She smiled sadly. "He was my husband. He had every right. You could do nothing."

Her words didn't assuage his guilt, but they fed his determination to make it up. "He's gone, you know. Make yourself believe it. If you let him continue to blight your existence, you give him power over you still. Don't do it. Flourish, instead. Your revenge will be *joie de vivre*."

A twist of her mouth almost looked like a smile.

"Disobey his every rule, Sylvia. Defy his every unreasonable dictate." He leaned his forehead to hers. "Fly free."

"Such as entertaining Lord Arthur's family?"

"Absolutely."

"But there's something about that woman, Catherine ..."

"Whatever it is, if it came from Emery, it is poison, and we will not let it blight our lives!"

She nodded, but Will wasn't convinced that she meant it.

When his sister shut the door, he slumped against the wall. She looked skeptical and, he suspected, afraid. Catherine's words came back to him. "Give her time." He couldn't undo eleven years of damage in a few months.

How am I to endure years of this? If he had to do it alone, he couldn't bear it.

For now, he had boys to oversee. *I need to remind them to hang mistletoe.* A smile took hold, and he stood a bit taller. He hurried to the family parlor.

8

N*ow for the hard part*, Will thought, when he entered the family parlor.

The Wheatlys' arrival had gone smoothly, primarily because Will had thrown the fear of God—or of being turned off—into Stowe. Lord Arthur looked relieved to be in the guest wing, where fewer memories haunted him. The boys greeted cots in the nursery with hoots of joy. Catherine looked merely resigned, until she saw that her room looked out over the gardens. He expected that, by morning, she would have drawn up plans to restore them.

Dinner also passed without incident. Lord Arthur remarked that he had few memories of the dining salon.

"I was seldom at home, you see, once I was an adult," he had said.

Stunned silence greeted that pronouncement, and Will once again offered a prayer of gratitude for Glenaire. The marquess diverted the discussion smoothly.

Both Sylvia and Catherine made a greater effort than they had at the previous dinner. Catherine's disinterest in fashion and Sylvia's distaste for crop rotation limited them, however, and only Glenaire's gambits kept the conversation flowing. When the ladies rose, they left the gentlemen to their port with no sign of animosity.

"That went well," Will mused, holding his crystal glass out for the footman to fill.

A rueful smile lit Glenaire's austere face. "I've had an easier time managing conversation at diplomatic dinners with the Prussians and French."

"I'm sorry, Chadbourn. Returning here will take some adjustment," Lord Arthur said.

"No apology necessary," Will said.

"Indeed not. I found the discussion about your research fascinating," Glenaire added. Will couldn't tell if the marquess was serious, but the remark, and the relief it brought to Lord Arthur's face, gratified him.

"My Catherine isn't used to this, but she managed it well."

"Your Catherine would grace any dinner, Lord Arthur." Will meant it. Her breeding showed in the very line of her wrist when she ate, in her tone of voice, and in her instinctive good manners.

The old man preened.

"Harrow for the Michaelmas term, is it?" Glenaire asked.

Lord Arthur worried his lower lip. "I fear so," he said at last.

"Don't fear it. It will serve them well," Glenaire answered.

"I can't tell you how relieved I am to send Charles off with his cousins. I went alone, and the first term felt like Hell." He and Glenaire caught eyes and let a happy memory pass between them.

"Friends matter. I agree," the marquess said. "You are blessed, both of you, to send them off with ready-made allies."

The conversation veered easily into remembered teachers, shared love—and distaste—for various subjects, and some of the happier times at school.

Will sent a footman to tell the boys they could join the family, and the three men rose. The earl felt satisfied with himself, until he put his hand to the door to the family parlor. Lord Arthur froze. He definitely had memories of the room they were about to enter, as he had made clear the last time.

Yes, now for the hard part.

~

CATHERINE ENJOYED A PRIVATE SMILE. One moment Sylvia stood, rigid and uncertain, near the doorway. The next, her son accosted her with a hug and an enthusiastic kiss. The duchess couldn't hold back a warm smile, but her expression reflected puzzlement and confusion. Charles grinned back and pointed up. *Those mischief-makers hung mistletoe where it will catch anyone coming in the door.*

Randy came in behind Charles. He looked apprehensive, but he stood on his toes to place a quick kiss on the duchess's cheek. "Joyeux Noël, Your Grace," he said, blushing furiously.

Freddy did the same, and the duchess allowed it.

Amazing.

Sylvia spun around, looking at Catherine as though to ask if the world had turned upside down. Before Catherine could speak, however, Glenaire came through the door.

Does a lady accost a gentleman under mistletoe? No power on earth could push Catherine to approach the aloof marquess. Her father followed behind, however, and she couldn't resist. "Happy Christmas, Papa," she said, with an affectionate kiss. The old man beamed back at her. "Happy Christmas, Daughter."

The sound of loud throat clearing came from the hallway. Lord Arthur stepped out of the way, to enable Will to enter. Catherine started to take a step back, but a firm hand took her wrist.

"Oh, no, you don't. Mistletoe rules," the earl laughed.

His mouth covered hers in a kiss that heated her to her toes, but managed to stay chaste enough for the audience. Catherine felt her world spin.

"Merry Christmas, Miss Wheatly," the earl whispered, searching her face. "I hope it is the happiest you've ever known." He released her hand, but not her heart. His eyes held hers. *What an odd thing to say.*

She felt relief when Will turned his eyes away to look at the dancing faces of three boys, and suggested they open gifts.

Songbird Cottage's modest gifts, framed watercolors, were well received. The duchess appeared touched by the pair of goldfinches in hers. "Chadbourn must have told you they are my favorite," she said.

"Actually, it was my idea," Charles said, proudly.

Will opened his gift to reveal a drawing of a humble English robin, head high. "I will treasure this," he murmured. Even the marquess seemed impressed with his painting of a sleek, black raven.

Once Lord Arthur thanked the earl and duchess for his pen set, all eyes turned to Catherine. "I can wait," she said. "I'm not sure the boys can."

The next moments were a riot of paper and exclamations. Freddy went into spasms of joy over a set of cavalry figures sized to match the miniature army in Charles's nursery. Randy grinned over a leather-bound copy of *A Guide for Young Shepherds*. Charles opened a copy of *The War of the Roses* and wrapped his uncle in an impulsive hug. Catherine initially suspected the duke could expect more luxurious gifts over the next twelve days, but doubt plagued her when Sylvia spoke.

"I've never known such a night in this house. Mistletoe, Chadbourn? Gifts?"

Pity filled Catherine. *Could it be, this woman had never had a holiday party?* Her father's next words wrung her heart.

"There never was a night like this. M'father didn't believe in celebrating. Church service, yes, but 'no pagan nonsense,' he would say." Lord Arthur sounded bitter. "I think the old man didn't want to spend a groat on family. It took my Mary to teach me how to make a family. Praise God for her." He smiled at Catherine sadly.

Silence greeted this statement. Even the boys looked at him, their expressions sad. Catherine couldn't find words. He had mourned her mother these five years, never more than at Christmas.

It was the duchess who spoke next. Her words startled Catherine. "Lord Arthur, you make her sound like a wonderful woman. Why did your father disapprove of her? Why was he so adamant we should avoid the pair of you?"

Lord Arthur glanced at Catherine and appeared to come to a decision. "May as well tell it all. Time to heal." He took a deep breath. Catherine saw Will and the marquess exchange glances.

Lord Arthur went on without noticing the others. "Mary had a child, of course, and wasn't married. She ran to Scotland when she knew she had conceived. She ran before I could stop her. It took me five years to find her, another four to set myself up to support her and Catherine, and a few more years to convince her. Would have stayed in Scotland, but all I had to offer, Songbird Cottage, lay right next to Eversham Hall. She hated coming back, but Emery let us be. Mary learned to love it."

Will spoke into the awkward silence, asking what they all wondered. "Lord Arthur, are you Catherine's natural father?" Catherine's heart cracked a little. She had wondered that very question much of her life. She wasn't sure she wanted to know, however, much less to find out in front of others.

Lord Arthur gave Catherine a look that widened the crack. "No. I wish I were. Emery forced Mary, the summer she turned sixteen."

The duchess gave a little cry. Catherine sank back into the settee. When Will came to sit next to her, she hardly noticed. Her attention belonged entirely to her father.

"Emery knew I loved Mary. He knew I planned to marry her. He did it to hurt me, but he almost destroyed her. M'father beat him when he found out what Emery did, but both of them wanted Mary gone. Wanted no shame on the Wheatly name, as if hiding her would cover what my brother did."

Catherine could not speak. When Will took her hand, she clung to his. She caught movement from the corner of her eye and saw Randy looking at Freddy as if asking for explanation. She had forgotten the boys were there. So, apparently had Lord Arthur.

All three boys had expressions filled with hurt and confusion. Concern for the boys brought Catherine out of her stupor. The boys obviously struggled to piece together what they had just heard.

Someone would have to give them blunt explanations she would rather they never had to hear. She glanced up at Will and saw the same concern in his eyes when he looked at his nephew.

Charles broke the thick silence. He seized on a boy's simplest issue. "Does that mean Cath is my sister?"

"But she's *our* sister," Freddy insisted.

"We'll need some time to sort this out, but I think you're both right," She managed to sound reassuring.

"Interesting!" Charles exclaimed. "Having a sister will be good, won't it?"

The adults laughed nervously and assured him that it would be.

Sylvia rose and bustled to the bell pull. "I think we need refreshments," she said, with a tight smile. Catherine could see that her hands shook. As sick as Catherine felt about what her own mother endured, she regretted that Sylvia had to endure yet more pain over the behavior of her despicable husband. *How on earth will I ever face her again? How can I face any of them?*

"I don't think I can manage food," Catherine said, rising. "You will understand I've had a shock, and I feel unwell. I'll bid you good night." She spoke rapidly and tried not to run out the door.

Will caught her as she reached the doorway. "Catherine, I know this is a shock, but isn't it better to know?"

She nodded, fighting tears and trying to tug free.

"We'll manage this fine. When we're married, it won't matter in the slightest."

Married? Merciful angels! She pulled free then and ran. She ran like her life depended on it. Perhaps it did.

"I THOUGHT I might find you here." Glenaire spoke as he sank into a leather chair in Eversham Hall's study, a male bastion of dark leather, lingering cigar smoke, and unread books.

Will grunted and drained another glass of brandy. He reached for the bottle and found it empty. "Ring for another one. There's a good fellow."

"Rather rushed your fences back there."

"I made a mull of it. Tomorrow, I have to go back to the beginning and court her all over again. She never even opened her gift."

"What was it?"

"Silk gloves, useless on a farm. I meant to tell her there's more to life than Songbird. That probably wouldn't have gone well, either."

"Did you follow her?"

"To her room? What do you take me for? The lady wanted to be alone."

"Did you at least tell her you love her?"

Will choked. "The Marble Marquess suggests sweet words of love to court a lady? I thought you believed love matches disgrace the participants and taint noble families with weakness."

Glenaire shrugged. "You want what you think your parents had: home, hearth, and love of the land. You don't need a dynastic marriage."

"Like you do?"

Glenaire acknowledged the truth with an inclination of his head.

"Oh, God, Will!" Sylvia burst into the men's refuge and threw herself at her brother. He hardly had time to register that she had called him by his Christian name, when she told him, "He's gone. Charles has run off!"

Chadbourn calmed her enough to get the story. She went up to the nursery to say goodnight to her son. "I mean to do it every night now. Emery said it made him weak but—"

"Easy, Sylvia. You went up, and then what?"

"His bed lay empty. And I found this." She waved a scrap of foolscap.

MOTHER, don't worry. Catherine ran away, and it is my job to protect her. I will find her and bring her back.

Charles

Will looked at Glenaire. "Catherine bolted. I have to go after her."

"Charles is out there in the dark, Will. You have to find him," Sylvia cried, clutching his lapels.

The marquess pulled Sylvia away from Will. "Go," he said. "I'll look after Her Grace." Glenaire grimaced while the duchess wept into his pristine neckcloth. "Shall we ring for tea, Your Grace?" he asked.

~

Catherine hugged Charles to herself. They stood in Songbird's barn, where Catherine helped rub down Lady Guinevere.

"You were brave to ride here, Charles."

"I had to. I *had* to. I didn't care if I fell. You ran away, and I had to tell you I'm glad you're my sister. *Glad*. Please give it time, Catherine. I promise to be a good brother. Maybe it won't be so bad to be my sister. Truly." In the damp night, his voice sounded thick and desperate.

"You thought I left because I didn't want to be your sister?"

"My father wasn't a good man. He did bad things. I don't blame you for being sorry he's your real papa." He swiped at his cheeks.

"Oh, Charles, that part doesn't matter. Your uncle Arthur is my real papa in every way that matters, and he's a very good man. I have a good life here at Songbird Cottage."

"You don't have to live at Eversham Hall! I'd rather live at Songbird, too. Do you think Lord Arthur would let me?"

Catherine smiled into the gloom. "Your mama needs you, I think. You've begun to make her smile again. You can visit, though, whenever you want, and I can visit the hall, too." *When Will isn't there. I won't be able to bear it when he is.*

"But, Cath," he said, and her smile deepened at his use of the boys' affectionate nickname, "Uncle Will likes you too. I know he does. I heard him tell Lord Arthur he wants you all to visit Chadbourn Park. I thought maybe... that is... don't people's families visit when people are betrothed?"

Oh, dear. She sighed deeply, and when she spoke, she meant the words for her own heart, as much as for her newfound brother. "Listen to me, Charles. Your Uncle Will is an earl."

"You are the daughter of a duke," he said stubbornly.

"You're old enough to understand that children born outside marriage are not well received in society. I'm called 'baseborn.'"

The boy started to speak, but she silenced him with a finger to his mouth. "Besides that, I have no dowry, no property, and no consequence to bring to marriage. Your Uncle Will needs a woman who brings prestige to Chadbourn Park. I can't." The bigger problem stuck in her throat. *He needs a woman who knows how to be a countess. I don't.*

Charles started, as if a sudden thought struck him. "Is that why you ran?"

"I didn't run. I just missed my home."

"You ran," he accused. "Uncle Will says only cowards run."

The sound of a carriage rattling down the lane interrupted them, followed by the sound of several people scrambling out.

"The house is dark. Randy, you check it anyway," a familiar voice called. "Freddy, look in the garden. I'll check the barn."

Will! She looked around frantically. "Charles, go tell your uncle all is well. Tell him I just need to be alone. Do it now."

The boy ran as if to obey, but she had no more than sunk deeper into the shadows when his voice, muffled by the slats of the door, reached her. "She's in the barn, Uncle Will. She thinks she wants to be alone, but I think you need to talk to her."

Catherine scrambled up the ladder to the loft, scooted through the stored hay, and sat against the wall. She pulled her knees up protectively. *I love him. God help me. I love him, but I can't face him.*

She heard the door open, and Will's firm tread pace the length of the barn, lantern light marking his progress. Silence followed, but her heart pounded so loudly, it echoed in her ears. She dropped her head to her knees and closed her eyes.

"Catherine," a soft voice said, startling her with its nearness. Will's head looked over the top of the ladder. He lifted the lantern and put it in the loft. The light flickering off his hair lit up the golden highlights. "Did I frighten you so badly? Did I go too fast?"

"You aren't thinking," she replied. "You can't marry me."

"Why not?" He pulled himself into the loft and placed the lantern securely on a nail that extended from a beam. "I'm unwed. I'm in possession of all my teeth and body parts. I can support a wife." He stood several feet from her.

"I am the baseborn daughter of a country scholar, who knows more about egg production than formal dinner etiquette."

"It's easier for you to learn how to set a table than for some society chit to learn egg production." He took a step closer.

She tried to scoot farther back, but the wall at her back held her in place. She scowled at his attempt at humor. "Your best friend is one of the most powerful men in England. His mother—"

"—is the worst sort of society dragon. I didn't let the Duchess of Sudbury tell me who to befriend when I was twelve, and I'm not about to start now. Neither does Glenaire. She means nothing."

He came two steps closer. "I love you," he whispered. "I've dared hope you return the sentiment."

"Of course I love you, you daft man. Who wouldn't? That doesn't signify."

"On the contrary, Catherine. It matters a great deal, so much, that nothing else does. If you can love my poor self, why can't you marry me?" In the lamplight, he looked like a puzzled boy, with tousled hair and a rumpled jacket.

His jacket! Her eyes widened when he removed it and tossed it on a pile of hay. She watched in fascination while he unwound his neckcloth, tossed it the same way, and stretched his neck and shoulders. "That's better," he said, coming closer. "Why, Catherine? Tell me the real reason." He took one more step, so that he stood so close he could reach down and touch her.

"I can't be a countess," she wailed. "I can't. You're an earl, and I can't be your countess." She couldn't take her eyes from the spot at his neck where his shirt gaped open. When he went down on one knee in front of her, her heart beat erratically.

"What—"

He put a finger to her mouth. "Quiet," he said firmly. He took her hand.

"Miss Wheatly, having established that you cannot marry an earl, may I ask you to marry a farmer? I'm a much better farmer than I am an earl."

She stared, open-mouthed.

"I beg you, Miss Wheatly. My two thousand acres, my under-producing hens, and my fading rose garden need you. I need you. I need a companion. I need a partner. I need a lover. Will you marry me?"

She swallowed hard. "Under-producing hens?"

"Badly," he said, his eyes holding hers. Lost in those eyes, she couldn't find her voice. Neither moved, until at last Will growled, "Damn it, Catherine," and pulled her to him. The movement unbalanced both of them, and they tumbled into the hay. His mouth found hers, and he kissed her hungrily. She ran her hands into his hair, but couldn't pull him close enough. She wanted to crawl inside him. She wanted to touch him everywhere at once. She wanted... him.

When he tore his mouth away, she whimpered and tried to connect her lips to his. "Say it," he demanded, pulling his head to the side. "Say 'I'll marry you, Will.'"

"I'll marry you, Will," she murmured, moving in to kiss him. She could feel his smile under her mouth.

Voices drifted through the loft window. "We need to test the angel part again, Randy. Get the goat," Freddy called.

"Do we use a pulley?" Charles asked.

When Will's hands began to move over her, reality faded away. Her last coherent thought was, *this time, Rosalinda the goat is on her own.* She sank into the love of her farmer earl.

The End

ABOUT THE AUTHOR

About the Author

Caroline Warfield grew up in a peripatetic army family and had a varied career (largely centered on libraries and technology) before retiring to the urban wilds of Eastern Pennsylvania. She is ever a traveler and adventurer, enamored of owls, books, history, and beautiful gardens (but not the act of gardening). She is married to a prince among men.

For more about Caroline

Website: http://www.carolinewarfield.com/
Newsletter: http://www.carolinewarfield.com/newsletter/ Facebook: https://www.facebook.com/carolinewarfield7/ Twitter: https://twitter.com/

OTHER BOOKS BY CAROLINE WARFIELD

The Children of Empire Series (1832-1840)

Three cousins torn apart by lies and deceit work their way back home from the far corners of empire.

***The Renegade Wife* (Randy's Story)**

A desperate woman on the run with her children finds shelter with a reclusive businessman in the Canadian wilderness. But now she's gone again. Can he save her before time runs out?

***The Reluctant Wife* (Fred's Story)**

A disgraced Bengal army officer finds himself responsible for two unexpected daughters and a headstrong, interfering,—but attractive—widow. This time, failure is not an option.

***The Unexpected Wife* (Charles's Story)**

The Duke of Murnane seeks escape in service to the crown in the drug ridden, contentious port of Canton, only to find his problems waiting at the end of the earth. Can love bring him back? (Available May, 2018)

The Dangerous Series (Regency Era)

Dangerous Works

A little Greek is one thing; the art of love is another. Only Andrew ever tried to teach Georgiana both.

Dangerous Weakness

A marquess who never loses control and a very independent woman spark conflict until revolution, politics, and pirates, force them to work together.

Dangerous Secrets

When Jamie fled to Rome to hide his shame he didn't expect a vicar's daughter and imp of a niece to take over his life. Will his secrets destroy their chance at love?

The Holiday Collection

Lady Charlotte's Christmas Vigil

Love is the best medicine and the sweetest things in life are worth the wait, especially at Christmastime in Venice for a stranded English Lady and a handsome physician.

An Open Heart

She may not celebrate the same holiday as others at the Regency house party, but the banker's daughter knows she can treasure her heritage and still reach out to people of different traditions. If only she can convince her beloved to have an open heart!

A Dangerous Nativity

With Christmas coming, can the Earl of Chadbourn repair his widowed sister's damaged estate, and far more damaged family? Dare he hope for love in the bargain?

(Prequel to both the Dangerous and Children of Empire series)

Anthologies

A Holiday in Bath

Holly and Hopeful Hearts

Never Too Late (November 2017)